CHARMING
THE BEAST

CYNTHIA
EDEN

Published by Hocus Pocus Publishing, Inc.

Cover art and design by: Pickyme/Patricia Schmitt

Proof-reading by: J. R. T. Editing

CHAPTER ONE

Chloe Quick was being hunted.

She glanced over shoulder, but the dark street behind her appeared empty. *Appearances can be deceiving.* Unfortunately, Chloe knew that fact all too well. She could feel someone in that darkness, watching her.

Every instinct she possessed screamed for Chloe to get out of there. She needed to find a safe place — fast. Preferably a place with a ton of people and some really, really bright lights.

But the street is empty! She rounded the next corner. Her nostrils flared. She could almost catch that wild, woodsy scent in the air. The scent of a beast. *I know you're out there, but you won't get me.*

Music pounded from up ahead, and her breath caught in her throat. Yes, yes, music meant safety! Music meant people! Probably a bar, and from the sound of things, the place wasn't too far away. She could go inside and vanish with the humans. Pretend to *be* human for just a little while —

"I've been looking for you…"

She froze.

Then Chloe heard the unmistakable sound of claws sliding over bricks — a sound that rather unfortunately resembled that of nails sliding down a chalkboard. Bone-chilling, as chilling as that man's deep voice, growling in the dark.

"You smell so sweet, little wolf…good enough to eat."

She didn't want to look over her shoulder. If she did, the street behind her wouldn't be empty any longer. *He'd* be there. And he might not even be alone. After all…his kind tended to hunt in packs. Chloe knew that a man wasn't hunting her in the darkness.

A werewolf was on her trail.

"Leave me alone," Chloe shouted, hoping she sounded brave and confident. She kept walking. The tap of her shoes seemed too loud.

So did the faint thud of his footsteps. He *wanted* her to know that he was closing in on her. Fear burned in Chloe's stomach. She'd thought she could escape.

She'd underestimated the number of monsters who waited in the night.

"You're going to be mine…*all mine.*"

The hell with that. Chloe decided to stop acting brave — she ran. She ran fast and hard and she turned into the nearest alley, hoping to be able to dodge and dive between the city streets and lose the jerk who was hunting her. She needed to —

A hard hand grabbed Chloe. She was yanked into the darkness. Pulled against a strong, muscled male body.

"This is what happens," Connor Marrok told her, his voice a low, lethal whisper in her ear, *"when you run from me. I have to deal with stupid shit like that fool out there."*

Her breath heaved from her lungs as relief swept through her. Connor wasn't there to kill her — he was the white knight. Well, a very, very tarnished knight.

"When I move my hand, don't scream."

Like she needed that warning. His hand slowly lowered, but Connor didn't let her go. He kept Chloe trapped between the bricks and his body. In the dark, his golden eyes gleamed down at her. Chloe's vision was sharp — unnaturally so — and she had no trouble discerning the hard lines of his face — his high cheekbones, his square jaw, that sharp blade of his nose, the oddly sexy cleft in his chin, his sensual lips, his —

"You just had to run from me, didn't you?"

"I got tired of being a prisoner," Chloe whispered. Her words were the truth. Sure, she'd been kept in a cabin, not a jail cell, but she'd still recognized the prison walls for what they were. And Connor — he was her jailer. A jailer in an unfortunately attractive package. Connor worked for the Seattle Para Unit and his job there — other than fighting the real-life monsters that most humans didn't even realize were out there — well, his job was to protect her.

To cage her.

"Baby, you don't even know the first thing about a real prison."

Her chin jutted up. Seriously, he thought her life had been all sunshine and lollipops? Bull. She knew pain. She knew hell.

She could teach him plenty about both.

"There is something fucking *wrong* with your scent," he told her, voice hard and rough. "You know that! I warned you days ago. I told you that if you went out, you'd attract every werewolf within a ten mile radius."

But she hadn't attracted Connor, and he was a werewolf. She knew it — she'd seen him change. His golden eyes had lit with the glow of his beast and he'd full-on shifted, right in front of her.

He can shift. I never could. No, she wasn't like him. Wasn't like any of the other werewolves that roamed the night.

"*Get away from her!*" That bellow came from the mouth of the alley. Her head turned and, sure enough, the hunter had found her.

"Hell." Connor pushed her behind his rather broad back. His hands were loose at his sides as he faced-off against the guy who was rushing toward them. "Buddy, you're going to want to stay back."

"I. Want. Her!"

She didn't even know who that fellow was! She inhaled, actually trying to smell herself and, yeah, okay, she could smell her strawberry body lotion, but that was it. She wasn't emitting some kind of werewolf pheromone beacon thing, was she? Chloe sniffed again. Still nothing.

"Too bad," Connor's voice was little more than a growl. The beast he carried must be close. "Because she's already taken."

Chloe used that moment to inch back a bit. Connor's focus stayed on the man before him.

"Never smelled a she-wolf like her!" The man advancing shouted, "*Want!*"

Uh, great, fabulous. "I'm not a she-wolf!" Chloe yelled, just to be clear. It was so sad that she had to actually yell things like that.

Chloe didn't live in blissful ignorance like most of the humans out there. She didn't just get to spend her days working and shopping and flirting with cute men. No, she had to know about the monsters out there — the werewolves and the vampires who often hid in plain sight. She knew far too much about them.

And had, since she'd been sixteen. Her life had changed in an instant when a werewolf pack had attacked her and her friend Olivia.

"I don't really give a shit what you want," Connor said to the other werewolf. Chloe was thinking of the other guy as the *hunter*. Because that was what he'd been doing...hunting her. "You're not getting her," Connor told him flatly.

The clouds parted and the light from the moon spilled down onto them. They were so lucky it wasn't a full moon. If it had been, those two men wouldn't have been talking at all. Their beasts would have taken over. There would have been teeth and claws and blood and death.

Werewolves had very little control when the moon was full.

Chloe peeked over Connor's shoulder. The moonlight fell on the hunter's blond hair. He was blond and fair, while Connor was dark, his thick hair a little too long as it brushed against his shoulders. Opposites in appearance, but both of these men were alike on the inside — they carried beasts, beasts that were ready to break loose.

"I don't want to kill you," the blond hunter told Connor. "But if you don't give me the woman, I will."

Connor just shrugged. *Shrugged.* "You can try to kill me," he said, almost sounding bored, "but it's not going to happen. This is the way things will go down. You'll come at me. I'll kick your ass without even having to go full shift. Then I'll walk away...with her." He took a step toward the blond. "Because I'm an alpha, asshole. And you just screwed with the wrong wolf."

Chloe retreated a bit more. It was wrong, yes, she knew it, but as soon as those two attacked each other, she was going to race out of there. She actually had no doubt that Connor could kick the other werewolf's ass, just as he'd said. After all, Connor *was* an alpha werewolf. They weren't exactly thick on the ground. He'd win the battle, then he'd come looking for her.

By that time, Chloe hoped to be long gone.

"You should save yourself some pain," Connor told the other guy. "Walk away now."

"*Her scent...*"

He was really freaking her out with all that scent talk. Her foot slipped over a discarded bottle. Chloe almost landed on her ass, but she righted herself at the last moment and—

The snap and pop of bones filled the air. The blond was transforming, going full-on wolf right then and there. She wanted to put her hands over her ears because Chloe *hated* the terrible sounds that came from a shift. Bones weren't meant to break and reshape that way. Nausea rolled in her belly even as the man hit the ground, landing not on his hands, but on his paws. Fur burst out from his skin and when he tilted back his head, a howl broke the night.

Good thing there aren't a ton of humans running around here.

The shifted wolf was lunging toward Connor. And, sure enough, Connor hadn't fully shifted. She'd already known that he didn't shift a lot. Probably because of the crazy control issue she'd noticed about him. *Connor always had to be in control.* But she could see that his nails had turned into razor-sharp claws. He kept those claws at his side, his body loose, too relaxed.

The charging werewolf came closer and closer —

I should run now. Connor is focused fully on the other wolf. I should run. But she didn't move because...

What if I'm wrong? What if Connor can't take this guy down? A trickle of fear shot through her blood. She bent, grabbed the bottle she'd tripped on and when the shifted werewolf — a big, white beast — collided with Connor, she slammed that bottle into the nearest wall, breaking off the bottom and making a pretty damn good weapon.

Only...Connor didn't need her and her make-shift weapon. As Chloe watched, he caught the werewolf — caught the guy mid-leap in the air. Connor's fingers — his claws — wrapped around the wolf's neck and Connor just held the beast as if he weighed nothing.

Alpha.

Then Connor threw the werewolf toward the nearest brick wall.

Right...*he doesn't need me.* Chloe started backing up. She kept her weapon though because, well, when a woman was being hunted by werewolves, she needed any arsenal she could get.

Connor was advancing on the fallen beast.

So Chloe turned and fled.

***

He heard the frantic thud of Chloe's retreating footsteps. Connor froze. *Not again.* His head turned, and he saw Chloe running fast, her black hair flying behind her. "Chloe," he gritted out as he started to give chase.

Then the jerk who just couldn't learn slammed into him. Connor's body crashed to the ground, the dirty, stinking ground of the alley. The werewolf jumped on top of Connor, and the beast's mouthful of sharp, dripping fangs went for Connor's throat.

Connor's hands flew up. His fingers locked around the wolf's snout. He clamped that mouth shut and glared at the beast. "You don't learn easily, do you?"

But then, the werewolf hadn't realized that he wasn't *just* dealing with another werewolf. He didn't know about Connor's enhancements. Mostly because few did.

"Listen to me, and listen well," Connor ordered. "She's not for you. If you come near her again, I'll do more than just break your jaw, got it?"

The wolf heaved in his hold.

Connor's hands twisted. The wolf howled, but this time, that cry was filled with pain because Connor had just broken the fool's jaw. While the wolf kept howling, Connor tossed the beast aside.

"Shift so you can start healing," Connor advised the wolf. A now cowering wolf. "And stay the hell away from what's mine. I don't care if she smells like strawberries and sex...don't ever stalk her again. Don't ever get close, got it? Because I've already claimed her."

When dealing with wolves, sometimes, you had to use a language they understood.

Connor rose to his feet. He lifted his claws. The wolf was slowly shifting in front of him.

"I said...*got it?*" Connor snapped out the words.

The man—a man now, not a beast—glared at Connor. But he nodded. He rubbed his jaw, then he turned and ran away. His naked ass flashed in the night because the fellow had shredded his clothes during the shift.

"Damn straight you need to run," Connor muttered after the guy because he was so not in the mood to be dealing with this shit.

He rolled back his shoulders and then stared at his claws. His beast was close to the surface, raised by the battle. It wouldn't take much to push him over the edge. To let that beast out. Because his werewolf...yeah, he'd caught the delectable scent that Chloe carried, too. A scent that was close to making him insane with need.

I'm just as bad as the rest of them. I warned her, but did she listen? Hell, no.

Guarding Chloe Quick was a thankless job. And if Eric Pate—the man in charge of the Para Unit—didn't control Connor's freedom, well, hell, he sure never would have agreed to take the job.

He turned, his head tilting as he gazed out at the night. He could still hear the faint pad of her footsteps. It was a good thing his senses were so strong. Good for him, but not so much for Chloe. He exhaled. She hadn't even stuck around to thank him.

His eyes narrowed. And he started hunting her again.

Connor ran fast, cutting right through the alley, following the thud of her footsteps and the faint scent that hung in the air. A scent that was pure Chloe. His heart beat faster—faster than it had when he'd been fighting that jerk—because the thrill of the hunt always excited his beast. Chloe knew that, she should have taken care. Her mistake.

CYNTHIA EDEN   14

He rounded the corner up ahead. The beat of music was getting louder. He could hear laughter. Voices. He saw that Chloe had nearly reached the bar. She probably thought that if she could just get inside, get to the humans, then he wouldn't follow her.

She was dead wrong.

But then, he wasn't going to give her the chance to reach them.

He could see her easily now. Just a few more feet, and she'd break free of the darkness that clung to the alleys and the nooks near the buildings. She'd be able to run out onto the street. Be right in front of the bar.

Not going to happen, baby.

He shot forward and grabbed her arm. But Chloe swung around, a broken bottle in her hand.

He growled.

She yelled.

He knocked that bottle right out of her hand. *I'm the one saving her ass...and she's trying to attack me?* Anger boiled within him. The bottle had crashed, splintered on the ground. He pushed Chloe up against the nearest wall. His hands wrapped around her wrists, and he penned them to the wall. "Is that really how you say thanks? By trying to cut me open?" He kept his voice low and he made sure to keep them in the shadows.

The last thing he wanted was some do-gooder human coming around.

Her breath panted out as she heaved in his hold. He didn't let her go.

"I...I didn't realize it was you."

Right. He could actually buy that. Seeing as how she kept having werewolves stalk her, she truly might have thought someone else was after her.

"It's me," he told her grimly. "You ran from *me*."

He could see every beautiful detail of her face, even in the darkness. He had perfect vision — perfectly enhanced vision. There was no missing the fear in her expression. He didn't like Chloe's fear. Even when he was pissed at her, Connor didn't want her to be afraid.

"You know I won't hurt you," he said, his voice a low rasp.

"Then let me go."

If only things were that simple. "I can't."

Her lips trembled. Her lips were the first thing he'd noticed about her — they were full and red. The kind of lips that instantly made him think of sex. Then he'd gotten caught in her eyes. No one should have eyes that blue. Maybe it was because her hair was so dark, a perfect black, and, in contrast to that darkness, her eyes appeared to be such a bright, electric blue.

Her face was heart-shaped, her cheekbones almost ridiculously high. She had a small nose and a slightly pointed chin. Her skin was pale, probably because the Para Unit had been keeping her in various stages of isolation and she hadn't exactly been free to roam in the outside world and soak up a bit of sunshine.

But that was what happened when you killed a man...and when you rose from the dead. *You get monitored by the Para Unit.*

Chloe Quick wasn't supposed to be in front of him. She'd died a few weeks ago. Not some near-death BS, either. She'd been knifed in the heart. She'd *died.*

Then she'd come back, thanks to the dark wish of a djinn. Only now, the Para Unit didn't exactly know what Chloe was.

"I warned you not to escape," he told her. The other werewolf had been right. Her scent was damn near intoxicating, and if he'd just been a werewolf, he probably would have been nearly mindless in his desire to claim her.

But he wasn't just a wolf, and that was why Eric Pate had given him guard duty with Chloe. *Because I'm supposed to be able to control my baser impulses.* But if that were truly the case, would he be holding her so carefully, his fingers sliding over her wrists, his body pushing ever closer to hers?

And would his cock be so heavy with arousal?

"I can disappear," Chloe promised him, her voice breathless. "Just give me a head start. I'll vanish and I promise, the Para Unit won't ever have to worry about me again."

Part of him wanted to let her go. It was her eyes...that gaze could make a man—or a paranormal—weak.

He didn't know exactly what end game Eric had planned for Chloe, but if Connor let her vanish, then he'd be the one paying for it. His freedom hinged on his doing this mission, and no one—not even a woman as sexy as she was—would stop him.

Connor shook his head. "No head start. You don't escape from me."

Then he heard footsteps—people approaching. Dammit. His head turned and he saw three men stumbling toward him. Their scents marked them as human, and in another instant, they'd see him and Chloe.

He felt Chloe tense against him. He knew she wasn't going to just let this opportunity pass by. She was going to scream and no doubt bring those drunken fools running. Then he'd just have to hurt them.

Before she could scream, before those fools could rush to her aid, he lowered his head, and he kissed her.

She bit his lip.

Deep inside, his wolf growled in pleasure.

Chloe, no, you know the beast likes things like that.

She strained against him. She opened her mouth, as if to scream even then—and his tongue swept inside.

He'd known for a while that he wanted her. Most men looked at Chloe Quick and wanted her. But until that moment, until he'd had his first taste of her, he hadn't realized just how truly dangerous she could be to him.

Because something happened. To him. To her. He felt her body stiffen, felt shock rock through them both. Because the desire that came right then—as he kissed her, as his tongue slid into her mouth and she actually fucking kissed him back—was unlike anything he'd felt before. It was as if a match had been ignited, and that small flame turned into an explosion, consuming him.

He couldn't get close enough to her. Couldn't kiss her deeply enough. His hands let hers go so that he could touch more of her. He had to touch her. His fingers curled around her waist, and he lifted her up against him. Chloe was so small and delicate compared to him. Chloe curled her legs around him, arching toward him. Her nails sank into his shoulders, and she kissed him with a fierce desire that matched his own.

His cock shoved against his zipper. He needed his jeans out of the way. Needed her naked so that he could thrust deep and hard into her. Needed—

"Get a room!" The shout was followed by drunken laughter.

His body tensed. Arousal and fury battled within him. *Need her. Want her...and they're in my way.* His thoughts were primal. Animalistic.

His head turned. He saw the three men, now just steps away.

"Fuck me," one muttered. "Am I drunk...*or are his eyes glowing?*"

A warning snarl broke from Connor. The three men turned then, and they ran away, screaming.

"Let. Me. Go," Chloe gritted out her order. She wasn't trying to desperately pull him close any longer. Now she was shoving against him. "Let me go," she said again. "Then tell me what the hell is wrong with me. Why did I just do that? With you?"

Slowly, he lowered her back to her feet, but he caught her left wrist, his fingers winding tightly around her. "The why is easy." His heart was racing and desire had him aching. "Because you want me and you've been fighting the urge to jump me from the moment we met."

She gasped. "I have not! I do not—"

"Save it, baby." He choked down his lust. For the moment. "We need to haul ass. Those drunk bozos will be back soon. Right now, they're shouting to anyone who will listen about the monster they just saw in the alley." He backed away from that wall, pulling her with him. "Now you either run with me, or I'll carry you away. But we are getting out of this place."

"You're the one who went all glowing eyes on them," she muttered, tugging against him. "I'm not—"

"Option two then," he decided. "I'll carry you." He could make better time that way. She wasn't equipped for super speed. Thanks to the Para Unit, he was.

She yelped when he hefted her over his shoulder, but then Connor was racing away, zipping through the maze of alleys and heading back for his motorcycle. The last thing he needed was to deal with a group of angry humans. Better to have an empty alley waiting when the three drunks returned with their reinforcements. Then everyone else would just think their story of a monster in the dark was total BS. The way everyone usually did when a monster story was being passed around.

In moments, he was back at his motorcycle. He lowered Chloe to her feet. Her glare seemed to singe. "I could have ran," she muttered. "You didn't have to turn me into a sack of potatoes!"

He hopped on the bike. Handed her the helmet. "Come on, baby. Time to haul ass."

"Stop calling me baby." She yanked the helmet away from him. "You don't mean it when you say it, so just stop. I'm not your baby, not your sweetheart. I'm nothing to you, and we both know it." Despite her angry words, she climbed on behind him. He noticed she was making an extra effort not to touch him. That wasn't going to work.

"Hold tight," Connor told her, his voice flat. "This will be one hell of a ride." Because he needed to get out of there fast—fast enough that any other werewolves who might be in the area wouldn't be able to follow them...or follow Chloe's scent.

He revved the engine. Her hands fluttered around his waist.

"Chloe..." Her name was a warning.

She slid closer. Her thighs curled around him, and her arms slipped around his waist. *Much, much better.*

He shot away from the curb. He thought he heard Chloe yell, and she definitely tightened her grip on him then. In fact, she started holding onto him as if her very life depended on him.

It was time she realized that fact.

He'd been assigned her case because his job was to make sure that Chloe Quick stayed alive. While the Para Unit might want her to keep breathing, his boss believed there were others out there who had far more sinister plans for Chloe.

The motorcycle whipped through the streets. And Chloe held tight to him.

**

He stepped into the shadows as the motorcycle roared away. Chloe Quick...his informant had been right. She was still in the Seattle area. Oh, that was certainly a huge mistake for the Para Unit. They should have taken her far away.

She might have been safe then.

Might have been.

Now, she was just easy prey. He pulled out his phone. His pack was stationed throughout the city. Eyes and ears everywhere. "They're on a motorcycle, heading north."

And the Para Agent called Connor was driving hell fast. No doubt, the alpha thought he could ditch any pursuers they might have.

But Connor was wrong. He hadn't counted on the fact that a full pack was hunting for Chloe. He didn't understand how important she was — *but I do.*

"Do not engage them," he said softly. Connor's motorcycle had already vanished in the distance. "Just follow them. When you find the safe house," the spot the Para Unit had been using to hide Chloe, "take up a position nearby and contact me." Because he had to plan his attack carefully. Chloe couldn't escape him.

Not when the full moon was getting so close. He had plans for Chloe and that moon. He'd waited too long to claim her. When that moon rose, when his beast surged with power, he would be mating her.

He ended the call. He heard the hard rasp of breathing and the shuffle of footsteps. A blond male ran toward him. The guy was rubbing his jaw.

His eyes narrowed on the man—the werewolf.

"That was one tough bastard," Wesley Green muttered. "Didn't even shift to fight me."

Interesting. Not surprising though, not given what he knew about Connor. "And he was still stronger, even in human form?"

Wesley nodded.

He didn't know if that information made Wesley especially pathetic or if it made Connor particularly dangerous.

"Never...never seen anything like him." Wesley yanked on his jaw. Bones cracked. "I think...think he's even stronger than you..."

Not possible. His eyes narrowed. "You were supposed to just follow Chloe. Didn't I give you that order?"

"But her scent...it was so sweet..."

He knew all about Chloe's scent, and that was one of the reasons he'd stayed back. Why he'd told the others not to engage. Chloe's father had manipulated her biology, nearly turning her into a perfect weapon. Her scent drove werewolves wild, and anything that wrecked a werewolf's control was very, very dangerous indeed.

"You're in my pack," he murmured. His...ever since the last alpha David Vincent, had been captured by Eric Pate and his Para Unit assholes. "So that means you follow my orders."

"But—"

He drove his claws into Wesley's chest. "There is no 'but' in this," he said. "Because of you, Chloe got away again. I'm the alpha of this pack..."

A gurgle slipped from Wesley's throat.

"You follow my orders," he said, and he twisted his claws, moving for maximum damage in the man's chest, "or you die."

His hand jerked back. Wesley fell to the ground. A big hole was where his heart had once been. But, just to make certain...

He pulled the gun from his waistband. Aimed right between Wesley's eyes. Those eyes were wide and terrified.

He fired, and the silver bullet exploded from his gun.

CHAPTER TWO

I kissed him! I kissed him — why in the hell did I kiss him?

Connor braked the motorcycle at the edge of the woods. They were once again back at her home away from home — courtesy of the Para Unit. A snug cabin in the woods, complete with twenty-four, seven guards.

Connor shoved down the kickstand.

She quickly pushed away from him and hopped off the bike. Her thighs were a little trembly after that insane drive, but she locked her knees and just rode out that quiver.

"Been wondering…" Connor murmured, his voice a low rumble. "Just how you made it all the way to town."

It had been easy enough. "I hitchhiked." She'd gotten incredibly lucky. After she'd run to the main road, she'd found a big rig cruising by. The driver had taken her close to the city, and, well, freedom had been at hand.

"Hitchhiked." He shook his head as he climbed off the bike.

She yanked off the helmet and tossed it to him.

Of course, he caught the helmet. Connor grabbed it in one of those too-fast moves of his. He stared down at the helmet a moment, then looked up at her. "You know, the wrong person could have picked you up."

"The risk was worth it," Chloe said as she turned away. She started marching toward her prison.

She'd taken about two steps when he grabbed her and spun her back around.

"*Dying* would have been worth it? I'm protecting you! That fool you ditched earlier—the one that Eric is probably going to fire from the Bureau—he was protecting you, too!"

Now she had to wince. Chloe had known it would be too hard to escape when Connor was keeping his too attentive eyes on her, so she'd waited until he'd gone to check in with his boss. While Connor was gone, a younger agent, a man named Harris Grey, kept tabs on Chloe. Unfortunately for Harris, he was only human. So he'd actually trusted Chloe and thought she was sleeping in her room and not, um…running wildly through the woods as she tried to escape.

"I would have thought dying once would be enough for you," he muttered, his eyes a golden fire in the dark.

But his words—they struck right to her heart and Chloe felt her own anger burn inside of her. "You don't know anything about dying or about what I want." She jerked away from him. "You're my jailer, right? Nothing more and nothing less."

And I shouldn't have kissed you! I should have clawed out your gorgeous eyes! But she hadn't. She'd pretty much been rubbing against him like a cat in heat.

Or a werewolf in heat.

They glared at each other.

"Don't ever kiss me again!" Chloe fired at him. "I have enough to deal with as it is! I don't need you—I just don't need you!" Then she spun around and started her furious march once again.

"Oh, baby…"

Her eyes closed. Why was his voice sexy?

"You definitely need me. And I've got the claw marks on my shoulders to prove it."

Her eyes flew opened. She glanced down at her hands. Saw the small nails there. Nails, not claws. Chloe kept walking. She heard him swear behind her, and then the thud of his footsteps followed her.

Chloe climbed up the rickety steps that led to the porch. Three of them. They squeaked beneath her feet. She reached for the door—

Harris yanked it open. His blond hair was mussed, as if he'd raked his fingers through it again and again. His brown eyes were stormy and his face—a fairly handsome face, but not that hard and sexy like Connor's—showed his fury. "If you're here for protection," he snapped at her, "you aren't supposed to run!" He stabbed his index finger toward Chloe. "We protect you! You aren't supposed to run from us!"

"Ah…" Chloe nodded and glanced over her shoulder at a watchful Connor. "He missed the memo, huh? Didn't get that whole part about me not being here willingly?" Well, now she didn't feel so bad about ditching him. She looked back at Harris. "It's not protection, it's prison. And inmates, well, they try to escape prison. It's just sort of what they do. A thing."

His mouth opened and closed, rather fish-like. She gave him a grim smile. "But I am sorry if you get in trouble." Those words slipped from her, utterly sincere. Harris had been good enough, as jailers went. She certainly didn't want the guy getting booted from the Para Unit because of her. "Maybe I can talk with Eric." *And while I'm having that talk, I can try and convince the guy to let me go.*

I mean, really…so a girl's father turns out to be an insane werewolf megalomaniac. Doesn't mean I'm like dear old daddy.

Her father's image flashed in her mind, and pain shot straight to Chloe's heart.

"Oh, I'm sure Eric will have plenty to say to you soon," Connor murmured. "For now, go inside and crash. You have to be dead on your feet."

Actually, she wasn't. That was the problem, right? She was supposed to be dead, only she was definitely back in the land of the living, even if she had been stabbed in the heart. *By my dad and then...then I turned on him.*

Only she didn't remember that particular attack.

Harris was still glaring at her. Obviously, he was more than a bit angry. Not that she blamed the guy. Not at all. "Sorry," she said. "Sorry for sneaking out while you were in the bathroom."

His glare got worse, and he flushed a deep crimson. Maybe she should have kept the bathroom part quiet. She slipped around him and headed back for her room. There was one bedroom in the place — hers. The men had been bunking on the couch, so at least she had a little privacy. She liked that privacy, especially when the nightmares came to her.

And they came every single time she closed her eyes.

Her steps were slow but certain as she headed to her room. Chloe kept her head down, hoping the pose made her look defeated, but...she wasn't.

I won't stay caged forever. She'd find a way out of this mess, sooner or later.

***

"What's Pate going to do to me?" Harris Grey asked, his Adam's apple bobbing. "I busted ass to get into the Para Unit. This shit matters to me!"

He'd busted ass, huh? Connor had gotten in a different way...mostly by attacking the Para Unit. Rather specifically, Connor had attacked his do-right brother Duncan, a guy who'd been human for far too many years.

Not anymore. Now Duncan is like me.

Connor had been on the wrong side in the battle with the Para Unit. Now, he was having to make amends for the deeds he'd done. Keeping Chloe alive? That was his current — and last — atonement.

"Can you...can you put in a good word with Pate? I mean, he likes you."

Connor laughed as he climbed up the stairs. They creaked beneath his weight. "I don't know if Eric Pate likes anyone." Maybe one person, his sister Holly. Everyone else? Not so much. Eric had a reputation for being cold as ice.

"But...but you've worked with him before."

Connor grunted. *Worked with him...been blackmailed by him...*same thing as far as Eric was concerned.

"This job matters to me." Harris straightened his shoulders. "Vamps killed my parents when I was thirteen. I know the monsters are out there. I want to stop them. I want to make a difference."

Right. Connor paused in front of the guy. "There's an important lesson that you've missed here. Those monsters you want to take down? They can look just like everyone else. Hell, they can even look like a sexy, little, dark-haired minx with big, blue eyes..." He looked over Harris's shoulder and saw that Chloe had turned back to look at him. She was gazing at him, her expression stricken. Hell. "Chloe—"

"Right." Harris nodded. "I forgot. She's not...human. She just—she looks so innocent, you know?"

Chloe turned on her heel. Went in the bedroom. Quietly shut the door.

"You always have to be on guard," Connor said. "Especially with the innocent ones." Then he slapped his hand on Harris's shoulder. "Go home. Get some rest. I've got the next twelve hours covered." Actually, he'd be keeping a twenty-four, seven watch from now on. Because, yeah, Eric was going to totally rip Harris a new one when he found out that the guy had let Chloe escape.

I got her back though. She's safe.

Harris looked relieved. "Thanks, man." He grabbed his bag and headed out. As Connor watched him go, he wondered...just how would the guy react if he knew he'd just been talking with one of the monsters out there? One of the beasts he wanted to stop?

The big, bad wolf.

That's me, all right.

Connor prowled around the little cabin. He secured the doors. Checked the front windows. He watched through the glass as Harris drove away. Then, there was just silence. The thick, engulfing silence that came from being far away from the city. That night, even the insects weren't chirping.

No sound at all.

He tensed.

Why aren't the insects making noise? He stared out into the darkness, but saw no threat.

He turned off the lights in the cabin and headed for the bedroom. The floor gave a faint creak beneath his feet.

***

His phone rang again. He'd left the town, left the body where it fell. Why not? He didn't care if Wesley was discovered. Let the cops find the body. Let the ME cut into him and see that monsters were horribly, terrifyingly real.

He was tired of being in the shadows. He and Senator Quick had made plans, so many plans. The monsters shouldn't have been in the dark anymore.

The senator also shouldn't have been dead.
Chloe has more fire inside than I realized.

He put the phone to his ear. "You have Chloe."

"We're watching the house right now."

A smile curved his lips.

"Looks like it's just her and that other wolf — Connor."

Connor Marrok was a problem that needed to be eliminated. Unfortunately, it wasn't always easy to eliminate an alpha. They could be frustratingly strong.

His pack member gave him directions to the location and ended, saying, "We're two hundred yards away. We won't close in, not until you arrive."

"Good." Because if the wolves got too close to Chloe, there would be no controlling them. Chaos would reign. It wasn't time for chaos, not yet. "I'll be there soon." He put the phone in his pocket. Looked up at the moon. Such a beautiful sight.

Had Connor enjoyed the moon that night? He certainly hoped so...because Connor would never live to see another one.

I've been planning to kill you for a long time, Marrok. The fact that the bastard was with Chloe now, well, that just meant the timeline for his death had been moved way, way up.

***

Chloe ditched her clothes. She shoved off her shoes and jeans and threw her shirt across the room. *He said I was a monster!* Damn him. Did Connor have any idea how much his words had hurt her?

She stood there, clad in her bra and panties, as rage and pain twisted inside her. Connor had no clue about her past. He didn't know what it had been like for her all those years. Not human, not werewolf. A freakish mixture of both.

The door opened. She whirled around, her hands automatically rising to cover herself in a sad and feeble attempt at modesty.

Connor stood in the doorway. It was dark behind him, and the darkness just made him look all the more menacing.

She'd never been attracted to dangerous men. Or at least, she hadn't, not until she'd met him. The guy was so much trouble.

Chloe notched up her chin. "You don't need to come in here and tell me to stay inside. I'm not planning on running, okay?"

He stalked into the room. Shut the door. That golden stare of his raked over her. Her skin actually seemed to warm as he looked at her.

"This isn't a peep show," she shot at him. Chloe grabbed for the sheet and wrapped it around her body. "And you can show some courtesy and *knock* when you enter a room. That's what normal people do."

He shrugged. "I've never been accused of being normal."

Her eyes narrowed on him and he just…kept stalking forward. Toward her. Toward the bed. "Wh-what are you doing?"

"After the stunt you pulled, did you really just think you'd be sleeping alone?"

"Yes, I did." He'd better not say—

"You're a flight risk now. To make sure that you don't try to escape through the window in the middle of the night, I have to stay close." His hand lifted and his knuckles skimmed down the side of her arm. "Very close."

She jerked away from him. "You are not sleeping in my bedroom!"

He nodded. "I figured I'd just sleep in the bed with you. Someone had to make the sacrifice."

What? *Sacrifice?* Her jaw dropped.

He smiled. Then he reached out his hand and turned off the lamp.

Her own hand flew out, fumbling as she tried to turn that light right back on. But he caught her fingers in his. Held her easily.

"This isn't happening," Chloe said. Why was her voice all husky? She cleared her throat and said, "You aren't staying in my bed!"

"I'm not saying we'll be fucking."

She was grateful for the darkness right then. She could feel the heat stinging her cheeks and knew that she'd flushed a dark red.

"But I have to make sure you don't run." His voice was a hard rumble. "You're my assignment. And unlike Harris, I won't be fooled by a pair of big, blue eyes."

Right. "Because you know I'm a monster." His words had hurt. Cut her to the quick. Mostly because…she felt like a monster. When she thought of the things she'd done, there was no denying her nature.

"You're my assignment," he said again. "Eric Pate wants you protected, and I'm here to make sure that you keep living."

Wonderful. *Jailer.*

"So climb into bed, close your eyes, and get some sleep."

Sleep would be impossible, especially if he was right next to her.

"I promise," he added as his fingers slid away from hers, "I won't touch you. I'll stay on my side of the bed and you can stay on yours."

Nothing he said reassured her. "I guess it's a good thing my magical, amazing scent doesn't work on you." She threw those words out deliberately to mock him and herself. Then she dropped her sheet and put her clothes right back on. She wasn't about to crawl into that bed with him, not just clothed in a bra and panties. "I mean, if the scent did the mojo like you've been telling me it does to other wolves, we'd be in trouble."

She climbed into the bed and slid as far to the right side as possible.

Connor lowered his body onto the mattress. It sagged beneath his weight, and Chloe almost rolled toward him. Her fingers clamped around the edge of the mattress and she held on tightly.

Moments passed in silence. All she could hear was the loud drumming of her heartbeat.

She closed her eyes, trying to shut out Connor, trying to pretend that he wasn't there. An impossible task, considering how hyper aware of him she was. His scent—rich, masculine—teased her nose and the heat from his body seemed to reach out and surround her.

"I never said that it didn't work on me."

Her eyes shot open. His voice had been such a low, deep growl.

"I never said your scent didn't influence me." She licked lips that had gone desert dry.

"If I were just a werewolf, I'd be on you right now." The mattress dipped a little more as he shifted toward her. "There's a reason Eric isn't sending any werewolf guards for you. You smell like fucking temptation."

Chloe shook her head. "I don't." She'd had werewolf guards in the past. No one had gone all crazy and said she was irresistible.

"Trust me, you do. After you…came back…something was different. I had to put two werewolves in the med ward at the Para Unit, because they were trying to get to you the first time you sauntered out of Eric's office."

Her fingers tightened around the bedcovers. "You're a werewolf. You don't—"

"You don't ever really want to know what I am."

Now that just made her curious. Her head turned on the pillow so that she could better see him. "Why did you kiss me?" Chloe hadn't meant to ask that question, but well, there it was. Hanging out there all awkward-like in the dark.

"I didn't want you screaming at the humans, trying to get them to help you."

She waited. He didn't say more. "You're such a liar."

Now his head turned toward her.

"I can tell when a man wants me." And there had been no missing his arousal. He'd definitely been game-on for her in that alley.

"I'm sure there have been plenty of men who want you." His voice sounded funny. Too tight. Too hard. Was he angry? Jealous? She couldn't be certain.

"Why is my scent different?" It was easier to talk with him in the dark. "Did I come back…wrong?" That was her fear. But then, she hadn't exactly been right before the change, either. At sixteen, she'd been bitten by a werewolf — several werewolves. She had the DNA that should have made her transform after that bite. Because once a human was bitten, there were only two options.

Death.

Or transformation.

Once upon a time, she'd had an ancestor who had been a natural-born werewolf, so Chloe should have transformed. She had, sort of.

Her beast had lived and breathed inside of her. She'd felt the elemental, the primal call from deep within. But when it came time to shift, she'd —

Gotten stuck.

A horrible mix of human and wolf. Not fully either. Stuck. In agony.

"You left me."

Chloe blinked.

"Right then, you just went somewhere else in your head. Where did you go, Chloe?"

Why not confess? "I think my beast is dead. I came back, but it didn't." Because she hadn't felt that primal call since she'd literally risen from the dead. Hadn't shifted — even in her stilted, painful way.

"I wouldn't be so sure of that," he murmured.

Like he would know about her pain. The guy was an alpha. Shifting wasn't a problem for him.

The guy could become a wolf in an instant. A blink.

"Eric ran his tests on me in that lab." Eric's sister Holly had been the doctor in charge there. Holly had poked and prodded Chloe until she had felt the urge to scream. Maybe she had — a time or twenty, mostly from the pain of all those experiments. Sometimes, it felt as if her whole life were one big experiment. "Do you know what he found?" Because Eric hadn't shared those results with her. He'd just sent her away — with Connor.

"According to his tests, you're a werewolf."

She flinched. "Then why don't I change?"

"The full moon hasn't been up since you rose."

Rose…what a nice way of saying *came back from the dead.*

"Let's see what happens then."

"And my scent?"

"Vampires can't detect it and neither can humans. Eric didn't even realize what was happening with you, not until I had to throw those other wolves against the wall."

She had to let go of her death grip on the bedcovers. "What does it mean?"

"Probably something very bad."

Fabulous. "That's the story of my life." She turned away from him. Closed her eyes. "Stay on your side of the bed, wolf, understand?"

"I hear you."

She tried to slow her breathing. Tried to pretend that Connor wasn't right beside her. Tried to pretend that she wasn't afraid of sleep.

"I hope the fire doesn't come," Chloe whispered.

"What?"

But she didn't speak again.

CHAPTER THREE

Chloe was asleep. Her breathing was deep and even and she was on top of him.

Every muscle in Connor's body was tight with tension. He'd been staying on his side of the bed, playing by the rules she'd thrown out, but, ten minutes into her little sleep routine, and Chloe had slid closer to him. Before he could do more than realize he was in trouble, she'd been on him. Her arms were draped around him and her head was snuggled over his heart.

Maybe he should have pushed her back to her side of the bed. If she woke up and saw them that way, Chloe would freak. But she wasn't awake right then, and she felt....good... against him. Warm and soft.

He hadn't exactly had a lot of softness in his life.

Not with his jerk of a father. A man who'd believed in giving as much pain as possible. A man who'd murdered Connor's mother, who'd made his life hell for so many years.

Until that old bastard was killed in Purgatory.
Right before Ian would have killed Connor, his
father had been taken out.

His hand lifted. He…stroked Chloe's hair.
For the first time in his life, he almost felt a sense
of peace slide through him. It was wrong. He
shouldn't be feeling peaceful, not with danger all
around, not with Chloe so close but—

I think Chloe is the one giving me peace.

That didn't make a bit of sense to him.

Still, he stroked her hair. He—

"*Help me…*" Her whisper. Low. Pain-filled.
"*It…hurts…*"

"Chloe?"

"F-fire…stop the fire…" Then she shuddered
against him.

His arms curled tighter around her. "Chloe,
wake up."

But she wasn't waking.

He slid her to the side, settling her on the
pillow there. He could see the tear tracks on her
cheeks. She was crying in her sleep, whimpering
as if she were being attacked.

This shit wasn't happening.

He leaned over her. "Chloe!" Connor
snapped out her name. "Wake up, *now!*"

She didn't.

His fingers curled around her shoulders.
"Chloe, wake up." Her tears were cutting into
him. He hated to see them sliding down her

cheeks. "You're having a bad dream." He shook her once, gently. "Wake up, baby, wake—"

Her eyes flew open. She stared up at him, and then she screamed.

He was pretty sure that his ear drums nearly burst, but he managed to smile down at her. "Glad you're back with me."

"Get off me!" Chloe shoved against him.

Connor moved back, but he didn't go far. He watched her, wary now.

Her hands were trembling as she touched her cheeks. She swiped away the tears. "I told you not to come on my side of the bed," Chloe muttered. "Did you listen? No…"

"Tell me about the dream."

Her shoulders stiffened. "What dream?"

Seriously? "The dream that had you crying. The dream about fire, Chloe."

She jumped from the bed. Paced to the window. Stood in front of the blinds. "I wasn't dreaming about fire." She tucked her hair behind her left ear.

His eyes narrowed. He'd been watching Chloe carefully over the last few days. She'd just given him one of her "tells"—when she lied, she tucked her hair behind her left ear.

He rose, but stayed near the bed. "You said 'fire' and you asked for help."

She didn't look at him. She lifted the blinds. Stared out into the night. "You're mistaken. I didn't—"

He could hear the whistle of the bullet coming. Rushing through the air. Coming so fast—and heading right for Chloe. Using his enhanced speed, he rushed toward her, he grabbed Chloe—

The bullet cut across his arm.

He pushed Chloe to the floor and covered her with his body. Her breath sawed out as she trembled beneath him.

"What in the hell just happened?" Chloe asked, her voice hushed.

"Someone took a shot at you." Only...that hadn't been a silver bullet. Not a wooden one, either. He knew how both of those bullets felt.

"But no one knows I'm here!"

"Correction, no one knew...then you went for a drive into town." And they must have been followed back. Sonofabitch. Connor had tried to be so careful.

I wasn't careful enough.

"Connor, I'm scared."

Those words pierced right into him. He lifted his head, just a bit, certainly not enough to present a target to whoever was out there shooting at them. Connor stared into Chloe's eyes. "Don't be. No one is going to hurt you." Not on his watch.

Because they'd have to go through him in order to get her.

From the corner of his eye, he spotted something gleaming on the wooden floor. He reached over and his fingers curled around the object—not a bullet, not a regular one anyway. It was… "A tranq," he muttered. "Hell, they're trying to take you in alive."

He could practically feel her fear filling the room.

"We have to get out of here, Chloe," Connor told her. Unfortunately, that wasn't going to be easy. "We're sitting ducks in this cabin. I'm not going to wait for them to close in on us."

"I thought this place was supposed to be safe! It's a *safe* house!"

And it should have been safe. The place was isolated, so he should have heard the approach of any unwelcome guests. He hadn't, though. *So that means paranormals are outside.* And since those paranormals were hunting Chloe…*werewolves.*

Her father had been involved with a particularly nasty pack in Seattle. A branch that had wanted to come from the shadows and take over the area. But the pack leader, David Vincent, was currently in Eric's custody. The last time Connor had seen the guy, David had been in a silver prison cell, curled up in a fetal position.

Did someone else take over the pack? He'd figure that out, later. For the moment..."I want you to stay at my side, every step of the way, got it?"

"How many are out there?" Chloe whispered.

He didn't know. He was just hoping it wasn't a full pack.

He reached under the bed and pulled out his weapons stash.

"Seriously?" Chloe said, her voice strained. "That was all under me? The whole time?"

He loaded the gun with silver bullets. He handed it to her. "If a werewolf comes at you—a werewolf that *isn't* me—don't be afraid to shoot."

Her fingers curled around the gun. He loaded another. And he took the silver knife with him, just in case.

"Stay close," he told her again. If he went out the front door, he had no doubt the not-so-welcome wagon would be waiting, but there could be eyes on the back door, too. *Damned if I do and damned if I don't.*

Good thing it took more than a bullet or two to slow him down.

They crept toward the front door.

"We're going for the motorcycle," he said. It was their best shot at freedom. "Run as fast as you can with me. We get on the bike, and we don't look back, got it?"

"Yes, yes, I've got it."

He braced his shoulders. Made sure to stand in front of her. "Don't be afraid to fire," Connor told her.

Then he yanked open that door.

***

Through his night vision binoculars, he saw Connor Marrok yank open the door to that sad little shack. He smiled. "Fill him with silver and take that bastard out."

Connor thought he was so big and bad, but even the bad asses fell.

"Make sure to only hit Chloe with the tranqs. Remember, do *not* close in. Stay back until I give the order." *Until Chloe is unconscious.*

He licked his lips as anticipation filled him. This was it. *His* moment. Finally.

The thunder of gunfire ripped through the night. Through those binoculars, he saw Connor's body jerk, just like a puppet on a string. Blood flew. A woman's scream echoed in the night.

How wonderfully perfect.

When Connor fell — and he'd be falling any moment — his men would have a perfect shot at Chloe.

I've been waiting for you, Chloe. It's time for your nightmares to end. I'm here.

***

Connor had just been shot! At least five—
six?—times! Chloe heard herself screaming, and
she couldn't stop. She couldn't—

"Didn't I say...to run?" Connor gritted out.

He was still on his feet. And he
was...shooting. Aiming that gun and shooting in
the dark. He'd sheathed the knife in some kind of
strap at his hip and he grabbed for her left hand.
Then they were running, but Connor kept his
body in front of hers, a giant shield to protect her.

More thunder. More bullets.

She bit her lip to hold back her screams. She
could smell silver in the air. Those bullets were
laced with silver—that should be a death
sentence for a werewolf, especially considering
the number of times that Connor had been hit.

The motorcycle was just steps ahead. They
were so close, but how was Connor supposed to
drive that thing? He was bleeding, had to be close
to collapsing.

More bullets thundered.

Connor grabbed her, pulled Chloe close, and
covered her with his body as the bullets slammed
into him.

***

"He's not going down," he barely breathed
the words. "That sonofabitch isn't going down."
And that was *impossible!* Connor had been hit

with enough silver to take out five alphas for shit's sake!

The guy was moving again, pulling Chloe with him toward that motorcycle. In a few moments, they'd be on that bike, and they would race away through the forest. Chloe would escape again.

Connor, what have you done to yourself?

But he knew. He knew too well. And the battle would be harder than he'd anticipated.

"Switch to the tranqs!" He barked into the phone. He knew his orders would be relayed to the pack. "If silver won't kill him, then maybe the drugs can knock them both out." Then they'd cut off Connor's head while he lay unconscious. "Fire, fire now! Do not let them get to that motorcycle."

"Should the men move in?"

Move in...close enough for Chloe's scent to tempt them? That was a risk. A huge one. But once the drugs hit her, her tempting scent would vanish. He knew the trigger for her tempting scent, just as he knew so many of her secrets. "Go in, but fire the tranqs every step of the way. Chloe Quick does not leave, do you understand? If she gets away, then fucking death will come. *Death*."

***

The motorcycle was right there! So close. Chloe saw Connor reach for the handlebars and —

Bullets hit him.

Connor jerked back, as he'd done before when he'd been hit. She grabbed for his arm.

Another bullet came at him and sank into his shoulder. Chloe could hear the frantic pounding of footsteps, racing toward them. Their attackers were coming out of the shadows.

Connor pulled her close. "Damn...drugs..." His voice was slurred and he seemed to slump against her. "Get on...cycle...get away."

More gunshots. He was hit again and his hold on her slipped.

"Get...away..."

Her right hand was still curled around the gun he'd given her. Connor had told her to fire if she saw other werewolves attacking. The men coming at her — they were *still* men. But she could see the glow of their eyes. Could hear their growls.

They were lifting their guns.

I'm sorry! Chloe fired. Once. Twice.

Two grunts filled the air and the men fell.

But others kept coming.

She fired again, and Chloe kept firing until the gun just clicked.

Moans and howls filled the air.

She dropped the gun and grabbed for Connor. "Come on! Connor, come on!" But he was a dead weight. No, no, this couldn't be happening! His eyes were closed and he looked as if he were sleeping.

Not dying, not dying... "Wake up!" Chloe yelled at him. They were at the motorcycle. They just had to get on and get out of there. "Please, Connor, please!" Because she couldn't just leave him. Whoever those men — werewolves — were, they'd already loaded him down with silver. Their intent was obviously to kill him and to —

A bullet sank into her shoulder. She looked down, oddly stunned because there was no pain. The wound just felt...cold. A deep, creeping coldness that slowly spread through her body. That coldness was weighing her down. Making Chloe want to just sag on the ground right next to Connor and sleep.

Sleep wouldn't hurt, right? There was nothing wrong with a little sleep.

"Got her!" Chloe heard someone yell.

When I sleep, the nightmares come. Fire. Screams.

Connor still had his gun. *And maybe it has bullets!* She fumbled and managed to grab it. Her fingers just didn't want to work properly, though, and she almost dropped the new gun. But she managed to raise it and —

A man with glowing eyes was right in front of her.

"You smell good enough to fucking eat," he said.

He had a gun in his hand.

Too bad for him, she did, too.

She fired. The silver bullet sank into his stomach and he stumbled back, yelling.

"Connor, get up!" She grabbed his shirt collar with her hand and hefted the guy toward the bike. She'd barely taken two stumbling steps when the shirt fabric ripped. Connor sagged against the ground. "No! Don't do this! I need you!"

She reached down for him again.

His hand flew up and his fingers locked around her wrist. His grip was steely, far harder than it had ever been before. Almost…painful.

"Connor?"

He pulled her wrist toward his mouth. His breath blew over her inner wrist as his lips parted.

"Connor, what are you—"

He bit her. She felt two fangs pierce her wrist, sinking into her veins, and she sucked in a breath to cry out. *No, werewolves don't do this! Not werewolves…*

He was drinking her blood.

Just like a…like a vampire.

She lifted her gun. Aimed it at him. "Stop." Her fingers were shaking. She didn't understand—he couldn't be a werewolf *and* a vampire. That just wasn't possible.

Was it?

"Pl-please, Connor. Stop!"

He pressed a kiss to her wrist. "Sorry…"

Then, in a flash, he'd taken the gun from her hand and leapt to his feet. Before she could even suck in another breath, he'd turned and fired that gun, shooting with perfect accuracy. When he hit his targets, she heard their pain-filled cries.

Her legs started to give way. That sinking cold had consumed her. The only place she felt warm—it was her wrist. The wrist he'd bitten. Before she hit the ground, Connor caught her in his arms. "I've got you," he told her. "It's okay now."

No, there was nothing about this scene that was *okay*.

He put her on the motorcycle. If he hadn't jumped on right behind her and wrapped his body around hers, she would have fallen off. But he was holding her too tightly, and there was no place for her to go.

"You're safe," he said.

She didn't feel safe.

The motorcycle's engine growled to life and the bike sprang forward. Connor wasn't heading toward the road. He was heading toward the thick line of trees to the right. Toward the forest.

She heard the howl of wolves. The snap of bones. Their attackers — those who still could, anyway — were shifting. Giving chase as beasts.

She should try to stop them. Were there more bullets in Connor's gun?

"Are you still with me?" Connor's voice sounded so strong.

She tried to speak, but her tongue felt thick in her mouth.

They were in the trees now. Branches hit her in the face, but she didn't even feel them. She couldn't seem to feel anything.

"Chloe?"

I'm with you. But…the words just wouldn't come and she couldn't keep her eyes open any longer. Inside, she was screaming. Begging for help.

Because she knew the fire waited in her dreams.

***

He drove deep into the woods, fast and far, and soon, he didn't hear the sound of the pursuing wolves any longer. But Connor didn't stop. He knew this area. Learning it had been part of his assignment. In case Chloe had ever been located by her enemies, he'd needed a plan to escape with her.

Only I almost didn't escape. Without her blood, I'd still be lying on the ground.

He cut hard to the left and zipped out of the trees. Chloe's head lolled back. She was out — they'd hit her with the tranqs and that pissed him off. He didn't know what those werewolves wanted from her, but whatever it was, they weren't going to get her.

Time for Plan B.

Eric had warned him that if things got out of hand, he would need to bring Chloe back in to one of the Para Unit's secret facilities. And if Chloe had thought she was in a prison before, well, that would be nothing compared to what was coming. But there wasn't a choice.

He hit the narrow dirt road up ahead. The motorcycle drove faster, faster…

She was so soft against him. He hated that he'd taken her blood. Even more, Connor hated that he'd liked that blood. Liked her taste. He'd wanted to take and take and take.

But then, he'd always known that he had a true monster inside of him. After all, he was his father's son.

Chloe had probably finally realized he wasn't the good guy. Not even close.

He kept driving. Eventually, the dirt road met up with an old highway. The sun began to rise in the sky and the darkness was pushed away. Chloe didn't wake up.

He drove.

His arm held her against his chest. His fangs were still out, long and aching.

He'd only taken from one other live source before—and that had been when he'd drank from a vampire. From Holly Jacobs. But he'd been in Purgatory then, and that had been a drink or die situation.

After that time, the blood had been carefully screened and prepared by Eric. He knew the dangers of taking Chloe's blood...he should *never* have drank from Chloe. Never. He'd been warned, time and again from Eric. Drinking from a live source was supposed to be forbidden. A dark path that he wasn't supposed to take.

But he'd sure as hell taken that path.

Now he wanted more. So much more.

"I'm sorry, Chloe." It was too bad that she couldn't hear those words. "We can't go back."

Would she be able to face what was coming her way?

He wanted more from Chloe. He wanted everything that she had to give.

But first, hell, first he was going to have to convince Chloe that he wasn't a monster.

Yeah, right. Good luck with that shit.

Because he wasn't just a werewolf, not just a vampire—he was an unholy combination of both. A creature forged from blood and death, and science. Science that probably should never have been used to build a new breed of beast.

He was a walking, talking boogeyman, and when she woke, he knew Chloe would probably run screaming…from him.

CHAPTER FOUR

"Chloe."

Her name pushed through the fog that seemed to surround her.

"Come on, Chloe, you're worrying me. You've been out way too long." She felt fingers stroking her cheek. "Open your eyes and look at me."

She was afraid to open her eyes. She knew that was Connor's voice, but where they actually were—what had happened to them—she was kind of confused about all that.

"You're safe," he told her, his voice almost gentle. "No one here is going to hurt you."

She cracked open one eye. Saw Connor leaning over her. His expression showed his worry. She cracked open her other eye.

He exhaled. "Good. I was starting to think they'd hit you with—"

Chloe shot up in the bed. It was an old bed, narrow, sagging, and Connor was right beside her. A *blood-covered* Connor was beside her. Her hands flew over his shirt. "You're hit! The silver—oh, Connor, you're—" Well, warm. Strong beneath her fingers. "You're...okay?"

"The silver didn't hurt me. I've healed."

Her head was pounding and her wrist ached. "But you're a werewolf."

He stared into her eyes.

She looked down at her left wrist. Saw the faint marks there. Two small circles. It was such a good thing she was in the bed then. Otherwise, Chloe thought she might have fallen. "You drank my blood."

There was a sudden, thick tension that seemed to cling to the air around him.

"Vampires drink blood," Chloe said with a hard shake of her head. "Vampires, not werewolves."

"There's something you should know." He rubbed his jaw. "I'm kind of a vampire."

She looked at him, then she cast a fast and frantic glance around the room. The place was small, non-descript. A bed, a table, two chairs, no windows. But there was a door, about five feet away. If she could lunge through that door, she'd have a fighting chance of getting away from him.

"And I'm kind of a werewolf," Connor continued in his oddly emotionless voice.

Her headache got so much worse. "You can't be both."

"Thanks to science....and vampire blood...I can be."

She flew off that bed and lunged for the door, but she didn't make it to freedom. Because Connor leapt in front of her, blocking Chloe's path.

He lifted his hands and said, "I need you to listen."

She needed a stake. Silver didn't work on him, so did that mean that a wooden stake would? She didn't know as much as she would have liked about vampires. Werewolves had always been her problem.

"The scent is back," he muttered. A muscle flexed in his jaw. "It's stronger than it was before."

"Okay, this obsession with my scent has *got* to end."

He stepped toward her.

She immediately slid back.

"Fear," he whispered and his eyes lit with understanding. "You weren't afraid when you were unconscious, so the scent wasn't there. You're terrified right now."

"Of course, I'm terrified! You're a vampire-wolf! Any sane person would be screaming right now!"

Connor winced. "Baby, you are screaming."

She grabbed for the chair near her and yanked it away from the table. Then she held it up, putting it in front of her. "Don't make me stab you in the heart."

His lips twitched. "With a chair?"

"With a *wooden* chair leg!"

Connor sighed. He didn't look frightened. He—

Flew toward her, tossed the chair against the wall, and yanked her against him.

She gaped at him.

His lips firmed and then he said, "Nothing has changed. My job was to protect you. I'm still doing that job. And I'm the same man, Chloe. The same man that I was two hours ago. The same man I was two days ago. The only difference is that now you know my secret."

She didn't want to know his secret.

He leaned over her. "If you'd stop being afraid, I would…I would have more control…" His breath blew lightly over her throat.

Oh, no. A vampire—and her throat? She shoved against his chest. "If you'd stop scaring me, then I wouldn't be afraid!"

"May I have…more?"

What? She shoved harder. "No! No, you cannot have more! I'm not your personal blood bank!"

"I've heard the bite can be…pleasurable."

She didn't know. She'd kind of been flipping out when he grabbed her wrist before. What with all the bullets and werewolves and the general terror that she'd felt.

"I want to give you pleasure, baby."

He was still way too close to her throat. Her heart was galloping like a race horse. Her knees were shaking and his teeth — they'd better not be growing.

"Connor —"

The door opened. It flew open and banged against the wall. Connor spun at once, pushing her behind his back. She was afraid she'd see a pack of foaming-at-the-mouth werewolves in that doorway, but...

A man stood there.

A man with blond hair. Blue eyes. A handsome face that didn't seem threatening at all. It *should* have seemed threatening because she knew that man.

Eric Pate. Leader of the FBI's Seattle Para Unit. And, if her father's whispers had been right, the man poised to take over the *entire* Para Division.

Eric looked at Connor. He looked at Chloe. He looked back at Connor. "Your fangs are out." Eric stepped into the room. "Tell me, *tell me* that you didn't drink from her."

"There wasn't a choice," Connor said. "She wouldn't leave me at the safe house —"

"Well, no," Chloe muttered, and she knew she sounded disgruntled. She felt that way, too. "I thought you'd die if I left you. You're welcome, by the way." Had he thanked her? No, he'd just taken her blood.

Connor slanted her a fast glance. Then he focused on Eric again. "The silver didn't slow me down, but then they hit me with tranqs. After the fourth dart hit, I went down. I would have stayed down, but Chloe was there. She reached for me and I...." His voice roughed. "I bit her."

Chloe waved her wrist at Eric. "Yes, he did. Right here, see it?"

But Eric was only looking at Connor. "You know what you've done? The drug we've been using on you might not work any longer. You've been so careful with the karahydrelene, but what the fuck happens now? We don't even know what she is!"

She wasn't the one who was some strange vampire and werewolf mix.

"They were trying to take her," Connor snapped back. "What did you want me to do? Let them have her? It was a pack — I'm guessing the remnants of David Vincent's pack. The guy was tied up with her father, and, now that Senator Quick is out of the way —"

Chloe flinched at the mention of her father.

"They're trying to get their hands on her."

Now Eric turned his attention on her. His gaze seemed so cold that she almost shivered.

"We don't know it was their pack," Eric murmured as he tilted his head to the side. He seemed to be considering things. She didn't really like it when Eric considered things. After a long moment, he nodded. "Connor, take a team back to the safe house. Search it. Find me a live wolf from that pack, and we'll make him talk. We'll find out just why she's suddenly so important to that group."

But Connor didn't exactly jump to do his boss's bidding. In fact, Chloe saw Connor's hands clench into fists. "And while I'm gone, what happens to her?"

"Holly is here. I called her in. She can run more tests."

More poking and prodding with needles? "I don't want more tests!"

Eric took another step toward her. "Do you want to be sent to Purgatory?"

Her blood completely iced. She knew what Purgatory was. Her father had mentioned it to her time and time again.

Purgatory was the only paranormal prison in the United States. Modeled after Alcatraz, it was supposed to be an inescapable strong-hold. Vampires and werewolves were carefully contained there. Werewolves were fitted with silver collars so that they could be controlled. Vampires were given drugged blood. From all accounts, the place was a living, breathing nightmare.

And Eric wanted to send her there? "Why?" Chloe whispered.

"You killed your father, Chloe," Eric said, his voice like the arctic. "There were plenty of witnesses to the crime."

Her lips parted to reply, but it was Connor who sprang forward. He stood toe-to-toe with Eric. "That bastard had just stabbed her in the heart. He'd *killed* her!"

"But Chloe didn't stay dead, did she? And we don't really know just how involved Chloe was with all of her father's...plans." Eric stepped around Connor. Stalked to Chloe. "I mean, were you involved with him? Working at his side every step of the way?"

Frantic, she shook her head.

But Eric said, "Your father wanted the paranormals to come out, to take over the cities, the world. He had grand plans, didn't he, Chloe? Only, you won't share those plans with us. You won't name the people who were working with your father. You won't give us any evidence to use."

She was shaking. Close to breaking apart. "I didn't help him! I never helped him!" She hadn't realized just how dangerous he was until the last few years. He'd...gotten worse. After she'd been attacked at sixteen, something had happened to him. He hadn't been horrified by the attack. He hadn't been sympathetic. He hadn't sworn vengeance.

I should have been the one to change! He'd been…jealous of what she'd nearly become. But when her shifts wouldn't work completely, her father had started to search desperately for a cure.

Not a cure to make her human again. A cure that would fully bring out her wolf.

And his. Because her father had wanted desperately to become an alpha werewolf. He'd had the DNA necessary for the transformation, so had she. But before he'd been willing to suffer the bite, he'd wanted to make absolutely sure…

That he didn't wind up like me.

"You lived with him."

He hadn't let her live anywhere else. She'd had guards every single moment, and that was why she wanted so desperately to escape Eric and the Para Unit. She didn't want her every moment tracked. She'd already lived through that hell for over ten years.

"You worked with him, on his campaign, on his projects at Capitol Hill."

"I did charitable work." Her father had thought the work made for good press. He'd never really given a damn about those she helped. He'd never really given a damn about her.

"You had twenty-four, seven access to him," Eric charged, "so don't lie to me and expect me to believe that you didn't—"

"She's not lying," Connor snarled at him. And, just like that, Connor was back to her side. His arm brushed against her. "Now back the fuck off, man. That's the last warning you'll get from me."

Eric blinked. She saw surprise flash over his face.

"Y-you can't send me to Purgatory," Chloe said. "I'm not a werewolf! I'd be dead within days."

"I'm not sure what you are." Eric's gaze swept over her. "That's the problem."

She inched a little closer to Connor. In that instant, she figured he was her safest best, vampire-wolf or not.

Eric's avid stare noted the movement. It almost looked as if he smiled. Almost — if that weak movement of his lips counted as a smile. "I gave you an order, Connor. I need you to get out to that safe house with a team, now. Try to pick up the scents before it's too late."

But Connor still wasn't jumping to obey Eric's orders.

"If I don't go?" Connor drawled. "Will you send me to Purgatory again?"

Again?

Eric's gaze darkened. "Your debt isn't paid."

Connor swore. "And she isn't to be hurt, got it? I'll go, but only if you fucking swear she stays safe until I get back here."

A muscle flexed in Eric's hard jaw.

"Not so much as a needle prick, understand?" Connor's voice seethed with fury. "No one touches her until I get back."

Oh, that sounded fair to her. A good plan. No needles. No touches. Nothing.

And Eric...nodded. "Bring me back a live wolf."

"Keep everyone away from her," Connor fired back.

"Deal."

Chloe's breath rushed out in a relieved sigh.

***

Ten minutes later, she wasn't feeling so relieved. Eric had just put her in a cell—a cell lined with silver bars. "This wasn't part of the deal!" Chloe yelled at him.

Connor was nowhere around. It was just her and Eric and he was *shrugging*.

"No one can touch you in there. You'll be safe in containment."

Containment?

She inched toward the silver bars. Would they hurt her if she touched them? Chloe was so sure her beast was dead. And, back when Eric had first been running his tests on her, he'd put silver against her skin.

Back then, it had done nothing.

But…what if something had changed? What if…?

"The cell is for your protection. Connor keeps telling us that your scent is acting as some kind of lure for werewolves. By putting you behind the silver bars, I'm ensuring that no werewolf can gain access and hurt you."

She'd realized — once she saw the cell — that she was in one of the secret Para bases. A place used for field work operations and for temporary containment of prisoners. "Are there other werewolves here?" Her voice came out softer than she'd intended. The area behind her cell was dark and she hadn't wanted to take her eyes off Eric long enough to look back there.

Eric stared at her with a guarded expression on his face. "People are never who we actually think they are."

What? That wasn't an answer to her question!

"Sit tight. Once Connor is back, we'll…revisit…your involvement in your father's business plans." He turned on his heel and headed for the exit.

She almost grabbed the bars. Fear held her back. "I wasn't involved!" Chloe yelled after him.

Eric didn't look back. He yanked open the door and headed outside. Chloe was left in her prison, a cot behind her and a toilet to the right.

She looked down at her hands. Saw her small nails. Nails, not claws. She hadn't been able to grow claws since her "death" at her father's hands. Was her werewolf truly dead?

She reached out to touch the bars. Her fingers were shaking. She should be fine. She hadn't burned before when Holly and Eric had tested her. She should be—

Her fingers curled around the silver.

Chloe screamed as her flesh burned.

***

Connor tensed. He glanced back at the Para Unit's base. From the outside, the place just looked like some rundown factory. Inside, well, that was where all the real action was.

"Problem?"

He turned at that voice—his brother's voice. Duncan was just a few feet away, studying him with a worried gaze. Connor had spent most of his life hating Duncan, blaming him for the hell that Connor had endured at their father's hands.

When it was all my own fault.

He'd originally hunted Duncan with the intent of destroying the guy's life, but then…well, shit, Duncan *was* his brother. Duncan was also one of those unfortunate true-blue types. It was because of Duncan that Connor wasn't rotting in Purgatory, though he probably belonged there.

Duncan had been the one to work out the deal with Eric.

In exchange for helping the Para Unit, Connor's past was being erased. A past that included a rather bloody pack life.

"Connor?" Duncan pressed. "What's wrong?"

"I thought I heard a scream." It shouldn't have been possible. He knew the walls to that building had been reinforced. The whole place was sound-proofed, but, for an instant, he could have sworn that he'd heard Chloe's cry.

Eric gave me his word. "Do you trust Eric Pate?" Connor demanded.

Duncan hesitated. "Well, I guess it depends."

Connor spun on his heel and started marching back toward the building.

"Hey, whoa! Wait, man, *wait*." Duncan rushed into his path. "This is about the Quick woman, isn't it? Look, she's safe. I heard Pate give the order. He was putting her in a containment area, but no one was getting close to her. You don't have to worry."

Then why was he worried?

"You know werewolves move fast," Duncan continued. "If we're going to catch their trail, we need to go, *now*. Hell, even with you and me out there, we may still lose their scent."

Because Duncan was exactly like Connor. Not just a werewolf, but more. Vampire. They had all of the strengths of both paranormal creatures. All of the strengths and none of the weaknesses, at least, according to Eric.

And that was why Connor could stand strong out in the sunlight. It didn't burn him. Silver didn't burn him, either.

"You ready?" Duncan pressed.

Connor cast one more look at the facility. He didn't hear any sounds from that building then. No more screams. "I'm ready."

But I'll be back, Chloe. He wasn't going to leave Chloe on her own.

***

"You lost her? Every single trace of her?"

He glared at the men in front of him. Fucking useless. If werewolves couldn't track, then who could?

"Sir, I—"

He fired a silver bullet into that werewolf's heart. The guy who'd foolishly tried to speak—he hit the ground.

"I don't want to hear excuses," he muttered, disgusted. "I told you that if Chloe wasn't caught, then death would follow." He'd given the idiots every single opportunity to follow his orders. They'd fanned out, hitting the woods, racing as beasts. "I mean, really, one alpha werewolf stopped you all?" Fucking unbelievable.

He raised the gun, preparing to fire at the next man. A blond male with dark brown eyes—angry eyes.

"I did my best!" The guy snarled. "That guy—something is off with him. You saw how many silver bullets we pumped into him, but he didn't go down, not until we started using the tranq…"

He lowered the gun. Yes, that had been interesting. *Is he more like me than I realized?*

"You should have told us what we were up against," the werewolf snarled at him. "You should have—"

He fired the gun. The guy howled and spun before he hit the dirt.

"*I* am your alpha. I don't have to explain anything to you. You follow my orders or you die."

"Alphas…don't have to…use guns…" The man on the ground—the unfortunately still alive man—spat. "Where are…your claws? F-fight…"

Oh, so the fool thought to challenge him? That wasn't going to happen. He aimed. Fired—

The bullet sank into the bastard on the ground. His rasping words stopped.

"I know where one of the agents went!" A smaller werewolf stepped forward. A man with stopping shoulders, a ladder-thin frame, and a big, slanting nose.

"I-I didn't try to follow the alpha," he confessed. A heavy southern drawl coated his words. "Figured the others were on him. I-I went after the human. The one here earlier."

Yes. Now this was intel he could use.

"Since the human was working with them, I thought he'd know where the alpha went when he raced away."

He holstered his gun. "You'll show me where the human is." What was that wolf's name? Bryant? Bennett? No, *Barrett.*

"I will," Barrett promised with a fast nod. "I will."

Then we'll find the human, and I'll make him tell me everything he knows.

Humans were so very easy to break.

***

Chloe waved her burning hand in the air. She could see the blisters on her skin. Big, red and — fading?

The blisters disappeared in seconds. The dark red burn turned a light pink.

She sat down, not on the little cot, but on the floor. She stared at her hands. *Silver burns, but I heal faster now.*

So much faster. What did that mean?

Only...she looked at her left wrist. The fang marks were still there. She hadn't healed from

Connor's bite. The marks were still just as bright, seeming to mark her skin. *His* mark.

Her hands curled around her knees as she hunched forward. She'd spent so much of her life afraid. Would the fear ever stop?

Maybe it never would. Death certainly hadn't slowed things down. She was still —

The lights flashed on above her. Too bright, blinding.

"*Chloe…*" Her name came from the area behind her cell. A shiver slid over her spine. "*I see you, Chloe…*"

Slowly, her body turned toward that voice. Now that all the lights were on, she could see that there were other cells back there. One of those cells was occupied by a man.

He was standing in a cell about twenty feet away. He wasn't touching his bars. He was just watching her.

"Do you remember me?" he asked her.

Chloe shook her head. Was she supposed to?

"That's right…we only met at the end, didn't we?" He laughed and she hated that grating sound. "Maybe I started by saying…I knew your father."

She jumped to her feet.

"I was the werewolf alpha he partnered with. The one who was helping him to cure *you*."

No, no, this couldn't be happening. Eric wouldn't have locked her up with that guy. *Would he?*

"I'm David Vincent," he whispered. "I was the alpha, until you and your fucking father ruined everything."

He lunged forward then and grabbed the bars. She thought he'd scream. She thought she'd smell the stench of burning flesh.

He didn't scream.

He didn't burn.

"*I was alpha!*" Now he was yelling and his words echoed in that cavernous space. "Until you and your father brought hell to my life! He promised me power...*and all I got was the death of my beast! My wolf is dead! Dead!*" He was jerking on his bars and yelling at the top of his lungs. "Now you...*you're going to be dead, too, bitch!*"

CHAPTER FIVE

The werewolves had cleared out. And they'd torched the safe house before they left. How fucking annoying of them.

"He's dead," one of the Para Agents said as he stood over the body of a werewolf. Connor knew the guy on the ground was a werewolf because his claws were out. At death, a werewolf's teeth and claws always came out. As if the beast inside had died too, but wanted to leave his mark on the world.

"He's dead…" Connor agreed as he inhaled…and then he turned to the right. "But that one isn't." He and Duncan raced ahead at the same moment, following that scent in the air. Blood and wolf. They exploded into the woods, rushed forward and saw the man. Staggering, bleeding…and not getting away.

"Stop!" Duncan yelled.

The man jerked but he kept going.

Duncan sighed. "What, does he think I'm going to fight his ass, werewolf to werewolf?" Duncan pulled out his gun. "They're not the only ones with tranqs. Hell, I think they got the tranq idea from us." And he fired. The tranq hit the fleeing werewolf and he stumbled.

Then fell.

Connor took his time closing in on the guy. One step. Another.

The werewolf rolled over to face him. And the guy...laughed. "They'll have...your man...by now..." He spat out blood. Someone had shot the guy with silver. A shot in the face and a shot in the chest. "Why do you...think...they left me? To...distract...wanted you...to follow me...not them." His eyes were sagging closed as the tranq pumped through him.

Connor grabbed the guy's shirt front and hauled him upright. The guy couldn't pass out, not yet. "Where did they go?"

"After...after the human...who was here...before..."

Fuck.

Connor kept one hand on the guy even as he reached for his phone. He had Eric on the line within two seconds. "Get a team over to Harris Grey's house, now. He's the target. They're going after *him*."

***

Connor raced hell fast to Harris Grey's house, but when he got there, Harris was long gone. The front door had been smashed in, and the small house was filled with broken furniture. Hell, there was even plenty of blood left behind. But no Harris.

He and Duncan chased the scent of the wolves for five miles, but then that scent vanished.

He glared at the scene around him. An airfield. Hell, yeah, that would explain the loss of their scent trail. There were choppers there, and it would have been too easy for the werewolves to just fly away with their prisoner.

"I'll start talking to folks, look for witnesses, get flight manifests," Duncan muttered. "The usual routine." He headed away with part of the team.

Connor nodded as his brother left, but he wasn't hopeful. It wasn't like werewolves would just tell everyone where they were going. This pack had power and pull—and they were using both right then.

He knew they'd taken Harris for a reason. They'd try to break the agent, try to make him share every bit of intel that he had on Connor and Eric and all those in the Para Unit. If Connor couldn't find Harris before the guy gave in to their torture…

Then we are all fucked.

And not in the good way.

***

By the time Connor returned to the Para Unit base, he was tired, pissed off, and more than ready to see Chloe. Every moment that he'd been gone, she'd been on his mind. He'd been out, searching for clues, but he kept thinking about her.

As a rule, he didn't obsess over any woman. His father had been obsessed with his mother—a sick, twisted obsession because his old man had been a sick, twisted bastard. Connor had never gotten close to a woman—well, other than for the occasional fuck. Emotionally, hell no, he hadn't let that weakness consume him.

After all, what woman wanted to be tied to a werewolf?

And…what if he was really as sick as his old man?

So he'd played it safe. Kept up the walls around him. No one had slipped past his guard, until *her*.

Chloe was always in his thoughts now. He felt as if she were consuming him. He wasn't even sure when the woman had gotten to him. When she'd slept in his arms? When she'd stood by him in the middle of that slaughter of a shoot-out and refused to leave him?

No one else has stood by me that way.

He needed to see her. Right then.

He dropped off his weapons and immediately started marching to the containment area. His first priority was to make sure she was safe and—

"Ah, now how did I know you'd go to her first?" Eric stepped from the shadows. "As opposed to, you know, debriefing with your supervisor like you're supposed to do after a mission? Does anyone care about protocol these days?"

He glared at Eric. Screw protocol. "I talked with you on the phone. Multiple times. I already told you everything I know."

Eric sighed. "Yes, you did, but I didn't tell *you* everything." He was blocking the containment area. "I, uh, agreed that no one would hurt Chloe…"

The bastard. Connor got a sinking feeling in his gut and he lunged forward. He grabbed Eric's shoulders and slammed the guy against the nearest wall. *"What did you do?"*

"I needed to see…how she'd react…to him." To him? *To him?* "Who?"

"You should ease your grip, I'm your supervisor—"

"Like I give a fuck!" He wasn't some trained agent. He was a criminal who'd been forced into this twisted web and Eric knew that shit. "What did you do to her?"

"She's unharmed." Eric didn't look even a little afraid. Annoyed, yes. Afraid? No. "She's in containment. She's just...not alone."

Connor shook his head. "Tell me you didn't—"

"David Vincent is in the cell next to her. I needed to see how she'd react to him. I needed to know if she'd been working with David. I was monitoring their conversation, listening for any clue that might give her away."

He wanted to pound his fist into Eric's face. "She has to be terrified," he said. And he hated for her to be afraid. "It's not good for her to be scared. When she's scared, her scent...it gets different. Even stronger."

"Yes, about that...I don't smell anything near her. Neither does Holly and neither—"

"You're not werewolves!" Connor shoved away from him. "And I'd already told you that she wasn't lying. She wasn't working with her father so she didn't know David Vincent. She didn't know anything about what the senator was doing—"

"How do you know that for certain?"

"Because she didn't tuck her hair behind her left ear!" Connor exploded.

"Right." Eric stared at him as if Connor had lost his mind. "That seals the deal. The woman is an angel. She didn't tuck back her hair."

He growled at the guy.

Eric raised his hands. "Easy. I might look human, but we know how deceptive appearances are," Eric said flatly.

Connor already knew that Eric wasn't human. He just didn't know *what* the guy was.

"Before you go for my throat with fangs or claws, how about you come into the observation room with me and just see what's happening in there, huh?"

His teeth were grinding together. "Fine," Connor gritted out. "But then I'm getting *her*."

"Someone sure seems to be getting attached to Chloe." Eric cocked a brow. "Are you quite certain that intriguing scent you keep mentioning — are you certain it's not working on you?"

It wasn't her scent driving him crazy. Well, part of it *was* her scent. But mostly, it was just *her*.

So Connor didn't answer the guy. He followed Eric into the observation room, though, and he stood behind the big window that looked out over the containment area. To those in containment, the window would look like a giant mirror. The prisoners couldn't see him and Eric because the view just went one way.

Eric leaned forward and pressed a button. Suddenly, the sound-proofing in containment was gone and Connor could hear —

"You should probably thank me," David Vincent said. He was pacing in his cell. Glaring at Chloe.

Connor really didn't like that prick.

Chloe sat on the floor of her cell. Her knees were drawn up near her chest and she'd wrapped her arms around her legs. Her head was down. Her shoulders were hunched. She looked defeated. Afraid.

"I mean, who do you think gave your dad all that werewolf blood to use on you? It's not like werewolves are willing test subjects, but I still made my pack give up those vials...for you."

"I didn't want the blood," Chloe said, her voice soft.

"The hell you didn't!" David shouted back at her. "You were stuck, caught in between two worlds. You wanted your beast to come out!"

"No." Chloe's head lifted. "How any times do I have to tell you? I just wanted to be human again, that was all."

"*I'm* human!" David grabbed the bars of his cell. He seemed to yank on them with all of his strength. "Because of that damn djinn friend of yours—Olivia Maddox killed my wolf and she made me human!"

Olivia Maddox. Yes, Connor knew her. And, once upon a time not so long ago, Olivia had been a djinn—a genie. But as they'd all learned, wishes from a djinn were very twisted things.

What a person truly wanted, well, he or she didn't always get.

Not too long ago, David Vincent had been attacking Olivia's lover, a vampire named Shane. David had been in werewolf form, and Olivia had made one wish...

I wish the beast would be a man.

And just like that, the werewolf inside of David Vincent had died. Only his human part had survived her wish.

Later, Olivia had made another wish...when Chloe's own father had attacked her, when Senator Donald Quick had been holding his daughter captive with a knife too near Chloe's heart, Olivia had wished...

I wish you'd let her go.

Chloe's father had immediately complied. Only, since it was a djinn's wish — and those wishes could go so very wrong — he'd let Chloe go by killing her. He'd immediately plunged his knife into her heart.

Then, according to the stories Connor had heard, Olivia had wished for Chloe to live.

She had. She'd come back from the dead. He'd arrived in time to see her rising — breathing — and so he'd been there when, moments later, Chloe fired a silver bullet right into her father's heart and killed him.

"My father's experiments made me worse," Chloe said now. "I never shifted fully and I...I felt like I was losing more of my humanity with each day that passed."

"Like humanity matters." David's lips curled in disgust. "He gave you enhancements that you don't even know about. Lucky bitch. You got the best one right at the end."

Eric leaned in closer to the mirror. "Now things are finally getting interesting."

Chloe stood. Connor saw her body tremble a bit. "What enhancements?"

David laughed. "Noticed anything...different...about yourself lately?"

"Other than the fact that I'm not rotting in a grave some place, you mean?"

His laughter faded. "I was supposed to get you."

Connor spun for the door. "I'm going in there. *Now.*"

"No!" Eric grabbed his arm. "Just wait, okay? She's safe. David Vincent can't hurt her. And this is the first time the guy has actually started talking. Hell, even when we used vamps, they couldn't break through to him. Probably some kind of damn alpha shit stopping them or maybe some *enhancement* crap that the senator worked. Either way, no compulsions have worked on the guy."

Connor didn't want to wait. He wanted to get Chloe out of there, right then.

But he looked back through that observation window.

"You don't...get...me," Chloe said haltingly. "I don't care what my father promised you." Her laughter was bitter. "And in case you didn't notice, he wasn't exactly the most trustworthy guy, despite what he said in his political commercials. He was probably planning to turn on you as soon as he got what he wanted."

Fury darkened David's face.

Chloe glared right back at him. "What are you going to do?" Chloe suddenly demanded, with her fists clenched. "We're both locked up here! You can't hurt me! You can't—"

"You don't have to worry about me. Your scent doesn't work on me, not anymore. It's the others you need to be thinking about..."

Chloe lunged toward the bars. She reached out—as if she'd touch them—but she yanked her hands back before they could make contact. "You know why they like my scent, don't you?"

"Oh, sweet thing, they like it because your father *made* them like it. He wanted you to be safe from the big, bad wolves out there. So every time you get afraid, that scent of yours is supposed to call on the beasts. You see, he thought they'd want to protect you. That the scent would mark you as one of us...so the pack would be there to keep harm from ever coming your way."

Chloe shook her head. "He...wanted to protect me?"

"Remembering that last injection he gave you now, aren't you? That's where the new scent comes from. But things didn't work out the way he planned, did they? Now when you get scared, you smell like prey. Sweet, delicious prey...and that scent of yours drives wolves into a frenzy. They don't want to protect you. They want to take you. To take and take and take until nothing is left."

Chloe clamped her hands over her ears, as if she could block out his words.

"Take and take!" David shouted at her. "That's what they'll do! I bet that new scent of yours really kicked in once you died. Because I'm sure nothing has ever scared you more than that. And that scent won't stop, not now that it's activated. The wolves will catch that scent. They'll follow it. They'll find you. They'll break you and nothing will be left — nothing — "

Yeah, screw going through the proper channels to get into containment. Connor's beast was clawing at his insides, fighting and demanding that he attack. So he just leapt right for that observation window. Eric's yell followed him as Connor shot through the glass. It broke, shattered, and rained down as he landed on the floor.

Chloe whirled toward him. There were tear tracks on her face.

And David Vincent — the bastard finally stopped his taunts.

That wasn't good enough.

Connor stalked toward David's cell. David smirked at him. "Did her scent pull you in, too? Like a bitch in heat, right? Want to break her, want to—"

Connor's hand flew through the bars. His fingers wrapped around David's throat and he yanked the guy forward, slamming David's head into the silver bars. "You're the one I want to break," Connor said softly. "You're the one I want to kill."

David was clawing at Connor's fingers, trying to get free. But David didn't have a werewolf's strength any longer, and he was no match for Connor. No match at all.

"I just need to snap your neck," Connor told him, "and you're done." So easy. One. Little. Snap.

"No, Connor."

Chloe's voice. Pushing through the rage that surrounded him.

"Don't kill him. Not like this, please."

David's face was starting to turn purple. Connor shoved the guy away. He turned to look at Chloe. She was near the bars of her cell, watching him with wide, desperate eyes. "You're not like him," she said softly to Connor. "You don't have to—"

David was laughing. "You're right…" He gasped out. "He's…even worse…"

The sonofabitch. Connor whirled back to him.

David scuttled out of his reach. "You think…I don't know…about you?" His words heaved out, as if speaking hurt him…probably because Connor had come far too close to crushing the guy's throat. "Word travels…in packs…know what your father did…know what you did…Purgatory…"

Connor felt a hand curl around his shoulder. He didn't look to that hand. He knew Eric was there. "Keep your control," Eric advised him as his hand tightened on Connor's shoulder.

Control is over-rated.

He wanted to shut David up before the guy said anything else.

Too late.

Because that asshole David said, "He's a killer…he's tortured…lied…destroyed…and you think he's…gonna…gonna help you? He's one…drawn to take…"

"Vincent is being transferred to another facility tomorrow," Eric promised Connor. "You won't ever see him again."

"I'd better not. If I do, he's dead." A simple truth, and Connor saw David shudder under the face of that threat. "Now let her out, Eric. Let her out!"

Eric pulled away from him. Connor watched as he went to the control board and typed in the passcode that would open the door to Chloe's cell. When she walked out, her steps seemed extra cautious, as if she were afraid of touching the silver.

"It burned her earlier," Eric said quietly. "So I guess her...sensitivity...to silver is back."

Chloe quickly came to Connor's side. "If that's back, what else will return?" Her face showed her worry. "I don't want to get stuck again. I don't want to be like that *ever* again."

He hated her fear. And her scent—damn David Vincent, but the guy had been right. Her scent pulled at him just as it did any other werewolf.

Only now that he'd had her blood, Connor found that he wanted her even more than before.

"Take me to the doctor," Chloe said. "To Holly. Let her run those tests of hers."

Wait, she was volunteering for tests?

"I don't want to go back...I can't live that way." Her lips trembled. "I won't. So get Holly to run her tests. Get her to help me. Please."

The desperate plea in her voice pierced through him. Connor looked at Eric, more than ready to trade, lie, threaten—do *anything* to get Chloe what she needed.

But Eric nodded. "Holly has been waiting for you."

And Connor realized that Eric had played Chloe like a pro. Exposing her to the silver, putting her with David...Eric had wanted Chloe to be afraid, to feel that the only people who could help her were the Para Agents.

Chloe had fallen right into Eric's trap, and, well, that just pissed Connor off.

I don't want him playing her. I don't want anyone hurting her. Not Chloe.

Because...she mattered too much to him.

***

She was poked. She was prodded. She was burned with silver.

But Chloe kept her lips clamped shut. She didn't cry out. She just let Dr. Holly Jacobs run every test that the woman wanted.

Her father had known about Holly. A woman who was supposed to be an expert on paranormal genetics. The senator had even tried to recruit Holly to help him in his research, but Holly had been firmly allied with the Para Unit.

Chloe wondered why Holly was so loyal to them.

Holly glanced up at Chloe, and the doctor's warm brown eyes were worried. "The sensitivity to silver has definitely returned."

Chloe almost smiled. "Yes, I noticed that, too." It was rather hard to miss the whole burning bit.

"A week ago, you had no silver sensitivity."

And she'd thought that she'd been free of her curse.

"Have you felt the urge to change? Your claws? Your teeth? Have you—"

"No changes, not even close." She rolled her shoulders. She was wearing a paper gown, one that she'd donned for her exam. "Not that my changes were ever anything spectacular, anyway. Getting stuck as a half-woman, half-wolf, well, that's more the thing of nightmares."

Sympathy flashed on Holly's face. Her dark hair was pulled back into a ponytail. "We need to monitor your changes. You *have* the DNA that should make you a candidate for the transformation, but something is—it's inhibiting you. I can't figure out what it is." She frowned down at Chloe's file. "Your dad injected you with so many different serums, I don't know if your own genetics are inhibiting the change or if it's something—"

"That he did to me?"

Grimly, Holly nodded.

"I just don't want to be a monster," Chloe whispered.

Silence.

She looked up and saw that Holly had a guarded expression on her face. "Well…" Holly finally said, her voice considering, "there are lots of different monsters in this world. And those monsters aren't all vampires and werewolves. Humans can be pretty screwed-up, too."

Holly turned away. Her shoulders sure looked stiff. Great. Chloe realized she'd just insulted the doctor. Probably alienated the one person who could help her. "You're…one of us, aren't you?" Chloe asked. It was just something in Holly's voice. Her tone.

Holly glanced back. Flashed fang. "I don't feel the urge to pretend as much any longer."

Chloe's heartbeat slammed into her chest. "You're a vampire." A vampire doc? How had Chloe missed that?

"That's what I am, now. Just as you—you're not human any longer. You have to accept that fact. Move on. Grieve for what you had, I did. But know that life isn't over. You can still be happy. You can still love and be loved."

Obviously Holly had never lived with Senator Donald Quick. Because Chloe had never actually felt loved. She'd been an appendage to him. The daughter to parade in public. Hell, half the time, she felt that she'd been his sympathy vote. *Look…the handsome senator is caring for his daughter…isn't it such a shame about what happened to his wife? To die so early, such a tragic, tragic accident.*

Accident, Chloe's ass. For the first eighteen years of her life, she'd thought her mom died in a car accident. A random, terrible accident caused by a drunk driver. Then she'd learned the truth. Her mother had been running away with her lover, leaving Chloe and the senator behind.

Only the senator didn't like to get left.

"Chloe?"

Her head snapped up. She'd gotten lost in her past and now Holly was frowning at her. "Chloe, I asked…those marks on your wrist…those are vampire bite marks, aren't they?"

Holly would know.

The door to the small lab opened. Connor stood there, frowning at them. "You about done, Holly?"

"That depends." Holly's head cocked as she studied him. "Want to tell me why you've been drinking from her?"

Chloe turned her wrist over. She tucked her loose hair behind her ear. "It's not a big deal. I offered my blood to him because he needed it." The doctor didn't need to know that Connor had been desperate and that he'd nearly scared her to death when he sank those fangs of his into her flesh.

"Connor..." Holly headed toward him. She put her hand on his shoulder. "You know the risk of taking from a live source. You have to be careful."

Chloe's eyes narrowed as she looked from the doc's hand to Connor's strong arm, then back again. Well, well, wasn't the doc awful familiar with her vampire-wolf guard?

Oh, hello...is this jealousy? Because it sure felt like it and she sure didn't enjoy that feeling.

Chloe jumped from the exam table. "I'll get dressed now." Despite the battery of tests, the doc hadn't given her any answers, at least, not yet. Maybe her blood work would turn up something they could use.

"I am careful," Connor said to Holly, his voice almost gentle. He'd never used that gentle tone with Chloe.

Jerk.

She grabbed her clothes. Marched to the changing area. If Connor was involved with the pretty doc, then he should *not* have gone for that kiss in the alley. The kiss had just made Chloe want...things.

You can still love and be loved.

Dammit. What was the doc? A greeting card?

She blinked away the stupid tears that wanted to fill her eyes. She changed behind the screen and heard the thud of footsteps heading to the door. The lab door squeaked when it opened and then closed.

Her spine sagged a bit as she stood behind the screen. She was on her own, Chloe knew that. The Para Agents would use her, then discard her when they were done. She could only hope she didn't wind up in Purgatory. She had to get away from Eric and his agents. Just vanish. Only then would she truly be safe. Only—

"Are you going to stay back there forever?" Connor asked.

Hell. *He* hadn't left. She poked her head out from behind the screen. He was standing near the door, his arms crossed over his chest, one dark brow cocked. His eyes—that gold was just too gorgeous, really—glinted at her. "Because I was starting to worry I would have to go back there and get you."

She was dressed. Mostly. Chloe slipped into her shoes and headed out to face him. She hoped her fear was hidden, but, hell, even if the fear didn't show on her face, he'd smell it.

He had too many advantages.

She was tired of that.

As she approached, he pushed away from the wall. He strode to meet her, and his hand lifted. His knuckles skimmed down her cheek. "I'm sorry," Connor said, surprising her, "I didn't know Eric was going to put you into containment with David Vincent. The guy's a dick."

"Who's a dick? Eric or David?"

"Both of them."

Her lips curved. He was right. They both were.

His gaze dropped to her mouth. "You don't do that often enough."

Her smile faltered.

His hand moved down a bit. His thumb slid over her bottom lip. "You should always smile."

And he should…he should move his hand because his touch was doing all kinds of *not* good things to her. Like making her heart race too fast. Making her breath come in pants. Making her want to open her mouth and suck his thumb.

Settle down!

She backed up. "You and Holly, you two are a thing, right? So how about you not get all touchy-feely with me and—"

He laughed. Chloe wasn't sure she'd ever heard him laugh, not a real laugh, anyway. His laugh was a deep, sexy rumble. His eyes crinkled, and what could have *almost* been a dimple flashed in his right cheek.

Trouble.

"Oh, baby, no. Just…no." He shook his head. "She's with my brother."

Shock stole her breath, then she sucked it back and demanded, "You have a brother?" There were *two* men like him running around?

She didn't know if the world was equipped for that. Chloe knew she wasn't.

"An older brother, one I hadn't seen in years. One I tried to kill." His laughter was gone. "But that's a story for another day."

It was a story for right then. "Seriously, Connor, you can't drop bombshells like that and just expect me to not ask questions. You tried to kill your brother?" Now she realized that maybe David hadn't just been bullshitting her back in containment. "Why?"

"Long story." He took a step toward her.

She almost retreated, but didn't. Her shoulders straightened.

"Maybe," he said, "when you trust me enough to tell me more about your past, then I'll tell you mine."

Her gaze searched his. "What do you want from me?"

"Right now, I want to kiss you."

Her breath came even faster.

"A real kiss, Chloe. Not one because someone is closing in and I don't want you screaming for help. I want a kiss that lets me taste you. A kiss that shows us both...do we really go fucking nuclear or was that all just from the adrenaline before? The heat of the moment?"

Fucking nuclear. She could admit, to herself, that she'd felt exactly that way in the alley. She'd been furious one moment and then nearly clawing at him in the next.

"No one else is here right now. Just you and me. I want a kiss, Chloe," he said again, his voice roughening a bit. "Will you kiss me?"

There were a million reasons why she shouldn't. Probably far more than a million.

And there was only one reason why she should.

Because I want him, the way I haven't wanted anyone in a very long time. No, the way I've never wanted anyone else.

She didn't answer Connor. Instead, she closed that last little bit of space between them. Chloe rose onto her tip toes, she curled her arms around his neck, pulling him toward her, and she kissed him. Their lips touched. One soft touch—

She was lost.

CHAPTER SIX

He'd never wanted a woman the way he wanted her. An insane, consuming, fucking, mind-blowing desire. Maybe Connor should have been cautious, careful, because of that wild need. Maybe he should have questioned it.

Her scent had been changed to lure in werewolves. What if the senator had done something else to her, too? What if the desire he felt wasn't real? What if—

Screw it. He didn't care. He just wanted her.

Her lips were on his, her body crushed to his, and he just needed her. Her mouth parted and her tongue swept over his lips. Hell, yes. His cock was already fully extended and rock hard, shoving at the front of his jeans. When she gave a little lick with her tongue...desire made him drunk.

He kissed her. Tasted her. Loved the way she felt against him. Loved the little moan that she made in the back of her throat.

Connor lifted Chloe into his arms. He took two steps and put her down on the exam table.

Her legs were parted, and he pushed between them. His hands curved over her jean-clad thighs. He wanted her jeans gone. He wanted to damn well feast on her. Every bit of her.

Her nails were digging into his arms, and Connor loved that bite of pain. It just made him ache for her all the more. Her head tipped back, and he put his mouth on her throat. Her blood was pounding so fast, right beneath his lips, his tongue. His teeth burned as they extended in his mouth. He wanted to pierce her flesh, right there, to take a few sweet drops of her blood.

When he'd first changed, the idea of ever drinking anyone's blood—straight from a throat, true vampire-style—had sickened him.

He wasn't feeling sick right then. He was fucking horny, and he wanted her.

His teeth raked over her neck. It would be so easy…so easy…

The door opened behind them. His nostrils flared as fury poured through him. *I was so close. So close and now—*

"Uh, yeah, I didn't expect this," Eric said as he cleared his throat. "I put you on guard duty because I thought you weren't influenced by that scent mumbo-jumbo…"

His hands tightened on Chloe's thighs. He looked up and into her eyes—such deep and beautiful eyes. Desire was in her gaze, but, now, so was confusion.

He figured it was time to get a few things straight. "I want Chloe."

She swallowed.

"Not because of her scent. Not because of her blood." He needed her to understand this. "Because she's…Chloe." *And she's going to be mine.*

"How about you step away from her now? Because I need you, *Agent*." Eric's voice had hardened. "We've got a problem, and I'm afraid the problem involves you and Chloe."

Her breathing was uneven. Her cheeks flushed. He needed to kiss her again. He wanted to do a whole lot more than just kiss her.

As soon as we're alone…

But he backed away, for the moment. Because no matter what Eric might be thinking, Connor still had his control. That was the difference between Connor and his father…Connor kept his beast in check.

I don't let the animal take the power.

When he backed away, Chloe closed her legs and jumped off the exam table. He stayed close to her because — shit, because he liked staying close to her. But when he looked over at Eric, Connor realized something was very wrong.

The guy's expression was even more tense than normal.

"You both need to come with me," Eric said. "Now."

Then Eric turned on his heel and headed out. Connor wanted to talk with Chloe, but he knew that this wasn't the time. He was aching for her, his jeans were way too tight around his cock, but something was going down. The sex he wanted with her — the awesome, mind-numbing sex they would have — it had to wait a bit. Fucking hell.

So he followed Eric, and Chloe was right at Connor's side. They entered Eric's office and Connor saw that Duncan was already waiting there. Duncan's face looked just as grim as Eric's.

This definitely wasn't good.

"We found Harris," Duncan said. He reached for the laptop on Eric's desk and turned it so the screen faced Connor. Duncan tapped the keyboard, and a video began to play.

"We have your agent."

In that video, Connor could clearly see that Harris was tied to a chair. The guy looked scared as all hell. Blood was on his face. On his shirt.

"OhmyGod…" Chloe leaned closer. "What's going on? What—"

"We'll trade him." That voice was coming from off-screen because the only person in the video was Harris. *"Give us Chloe Quick and you can get your agent back."*

Fury burned in Connor's blood. His fangs were out and so were his claws.

"If you don't deliver her, you'll get the human back in pieces."

Chloe shook her head. "I-I think I know that voice."

What? But, before he could question her, another man moved into the scene. A man with wide shoulders and dark hair. A man with claws sprouting from his fingers. He drove those claws into Harris's side. Behind his gag, Harris screamed.

The dark-haired man turned to look at the camera. "*In pieces,*" he said again. "Bring her to the Eclipse, be there at midnight...*or we start cutting off parts of the human.*"

Harris was yanking against his ropes, obviously trying to talk but the video stopped.

"That's the problem," Eric said. "A big fucking one."

"I know that man," Chloe whispered.

All eyes went right to her.

She wrapped her arms around her stomach. "The man who hurt Harris. I know him. He—I met him at my father's office."

"A name," Eric said. "Give us—"

"Keegan," she seemed to barely breathe the name. "He said...he was Keegan James."

Eric pointed to Duncan. "The werewolf we recovered at the safe house—get him. Make him tell you every single thing he knows about this Keegan." Then he looked at Chloe. "And you tell me everything you know."

But Chloe shook her head. "His name is all I know." Her hand lifted. She tucked her hair behind her left ear. "Just his name, nothing more."

Eric's gaze had noted that movement. His stare slid toward Connor.

Connor's muscle locked down because he knew that Eric was about to say —

"Connor, make her tell you everything she knows."

***

Harris had been tortured. *Tortured.* He'd been bleeding and Keegan had driven his claws into the guy.

Chloe paced the small quarters that she'd been given. Bonus for her, she wasn't back in a silver jail cell. Instead, she'd been returned to the first room she'd been given at the base, the room she'd awoken in hours before. The narrow bed was still there. So was the table. The chairs — well, the chair she'd threatened to use on Connor was still tossed on the floor.

She paced back and forth, her mind spinning. She had no idea what the Eclipse was, but midnight would be there all too soon, and Chloe figured she'd be finding out all about the place real fast.

I'm not going to let Harris die for me.

Whatever Keegan wanted, well, she'd face him.

She just wondered when the guy had turned into such a complete psychotic jerk. Maybe he always had been, though, and she hadn't even realized it. Maybe —

The door opened. Connor was there, filling that doorway. His broad shoulders brushed each side of the door frame.

As soon as she saw him, heat swept through her. Her reaction to Connor was just way beyond normal. Surely it wasn't healthy — or safe — to want a man as much as she wanted him? Especially when the man in question came equipped with both claws and vampire fangs?

He stepped into the room. The small space suddenly got even smaller.

His gaze swept over her face. A muscle jerked in his jaw, and he turned and shut the door behind him. That faint click made her jump.

"You lied to me, Chloe."

Connor, make her tell you everything she knows.

"I can tell when you lie."

She wished that she could tell when he was lying. It would sure make things a whole lot easier for her.

"What do you know about Keegan?"

She turned to face the bed. "He met with my father. Since he had claws in the video, well, I'm taking that to mean he's a werewolf." Keegan had *not* shared that fact with her before. But surely he must have known what she was?

"According to the intel that Duncan just got from the werewolf we brought in, Keegan is the alpha of his pack."

Alpha. Crap.

"Not only that…but it seems that pack used to belong to none other than David Vincent."

Her eyes squeezed shut. *Things just keep getting worse and worse.* "I didn't know that. I didn't even know Keegan was a werewolf until a few minutes ago." But now she had that horrifying image of him seared into her head. Nausea swirled in her stomach.

"With David out of the picture, Keegan took over the pack. According to the werewolf we've got—a real chatty bastard named Dennis who apparently didn't like being shot in the face— Keegan is one sick sonofabitch. And guess who he has a complete and total fixation on?"

She licked lips that had gone desert dry. "Since he wants me in the trade, I'll just assume that fixation kind of centers of me."

"Kind of," he muttered back.

She whirled to face him. "I didn't know!"

He stared back at her. "Dennis said Keegan has been killing members of his own pack. If they don't follow orders, he takes them down immediately. Sure seems like this guy is a real charmer."

"I. Didn't. Know!" Did he want her to write it in blood? To swear on her soul? "He was a guy I met at my dad's office one day. He was wearing a three piece suit, not sporting claws! It's not like you can just look and instantly say…" She snapped her fingers. "Werewolf! You don't know until the person shifts. I just…I thought he was normal." He'd *seemed* so incredibly normal. "When he asked me out for coffee…" And this was one of the most humiliating parts, but she forced herself to say, "I was just happy a normal guy wanted to go out with me…me, the freak who was so far from normal."

Connor's eyes began to glow.

Uh, oh. "Connor?" She inched back a bit.

"You dated him."

He made those words sound like the worst crime ever. Her spine stiffened. "We met for coffee, and, yes, after that, we went out a few times." With a sinking heart, she now understood why her father had seemed happy that she was going out with Keegan. Not because he'd been some up and coming young politician like she'd assumed. But because he'd been a werewolf.

Her father had probably been imagining werewolf babies running all around.

Oh, God…this is why my dad messed with my scent! He wanted Keegan to fall for me! Her father had given her the last injection after her third date with Keegan.

Her dad hadn't realized that was her *last* date with the guy.

"You *dated* him?" Connor took another step toward her and shook his head, as if the thought were truly mind boggling.

"I didn't know! Okay? It was just a few times. I didn't—didn't feel a real spark or connection, and I broke it off with him." She waved her hands in the air. "Then, you know, things kind of went to hell. I found out that my dad had been working to take out the Para Unit. He was trying to push all the wolves to attack, and I was just trying to stay alive."

Then things had reached an explosive level. Her father had died, and Chloe had lost everything she'd had.

Including my sanity? Some nights, it sure felt that way. *Because I killed him. My father didn't just die. I killed him. I shot my own father and I don't even remember doing it.*

"Did you fuck Keegan, too?"

His words were low, lethal, and absolutely designed to enrage her—Chloe was sure of it. Her hands immediately fisted to her sides. "How is that relevant?"

"It's relevant, believe me. The guy kidnapped a federal agent. He's stalking you, doing anything to get you back...so I have to wonder...did you have sex with the guy?"

But there was such a banked rage in his eyes. She could see it. "Jealous?" *Wait, no, I didn't mean to say that, did I?*

Everything was so screwed up.

"No." She shook her head as her breath expelled in a hard rush. "No, I didn't have sex with him. Things never got that far. It was only a few dates, so I have no idea why the guy is freaking out and stalking me." But this was more than just stalking. He was killing.

"Yes..." Connor hissed the word.

She frowned at him. Yes, what?

"I'm fucking jealous. I already hated the bastard as soon as I saw what he was doing to Harris. But to know that Keegan was close to having you..." His eyes glowed brighter with the fury of his beast. "I want to rip him apart."

She exhaled slowly. "Why do I feel like this is the first time you've, um, been jealous?"

"Because it is!" Those words exploded from him. "The first time in my entire life!"

"Sucks, doesn't it?"

"You have no idea..." He gritted out the words. "I will *never* be like him."

"Wait, you think you're like Keegan? Um, you're not, Connor. I could never imagine you hurting—"

"Not him. My father."

"What?"

"He was a sick, twisted psychopath. He said he loved my mother, but he was obsessed. He couldn't let her go, not even when she tried to run. And she did run, Chloe. She ran again and again. She took me and my brother and fled with us. But he kept coming after her." He paused. "It's not easy to escape a werewolf, especially when you're a human and the alpha wolf has your scent."

She reached out to him. "Connor, I'm sorry." Her fingers curled around his arm. His muscles were rock hard beneath her touch.

"The last time he found us...she put me and my brother in a closet. She was trying to hide us, and she was terrified. I can remember seeing the tears on her face. She wanted us to stay quiet. My mom...she said if we stayed quiet, we'd stay safe."

She didn't want to hear the rest of this story.

"I was so young, so damn little, and I didn't like the dark." His voice had gone hollow, all of the emotion bleeding away. "I ran out. I-I screamed. He found me. He found me and mom, and then he killed her right there."

She didn't just hold onto his arm then. She threw her body against his and held tight. His voice was so emotionless, but Chloe could feel his pain. "I'm so sorry, Connor."

"It was my fault. If I'd just kept my mouth shut. If I'd stayed in the dark..."

"No!" She was adamant. "You were a child. Anything that happened...*that was on your father.* You didn't cause her death! You didn't!" She tilted her head back so she could stare into his eyes. "Connor, you're a good person. You've helped me all along. Put yourself at risk and—"

"David Vincent was right about me."

"Stop it," Chloe whispered. She didn't let him go.

"I spent my life in my father's pack. That Keegan bastard has nothing on my old man. I saw things..." He shook his head. "I'll never be able to forget them. And my father couldn't abide a weak son. He was determined to make me stronger, no matter what." He backed away from her. "Ian McGuire didn't raise the weak. He killed the weak."

She wanted to reach out to him again.

"When I got away from that bastard, I changed my last name. Went back to using my mom's name, Marrok. *Because I wanted nothing of his.* But I couldn't escape him. Not really. I've always carried his mark on me." Connor lifted his shirt. He stripped it over his head and threw it to the floor. The light hit him then, falling right on his powerful chest. The muscles rippled. The muscles, the golden skin, and the scars...

So many scars.

"Werewolves can heal, so can vampires, but my father marked me when I was still a child, long before my first shift."

She had to blink away tears.

"Every time I didn't fall in line, every time I fought, every time I tried to get away, he'd use his claws."

There were so many scars on him. Too many to count.

"When I stopped fighting him, when I acted like the fucking *psychotic* wolf he wanted me to be, he stopped peeling my flesh away."

"Stop," she whispered.

He didn't. "When I was his wolf, I did things I never want to think about." He swallowed. "But one day, one fucking day, I got away. I left him. I was alpha on my own, and I wasn't ever going to bow down to anyone again."

"What happened to him?"

"Don't you know?"

She waited, wanting him to tell her.

"From what we can tell, he was in on the plot with your father. Senator Quick was rounding up as many werewolf allies as he could get. Purgatory was originally a set-up. Quick *wanted* the most powerful paranormals brought together because he planned to use them all. My sick old man was another of Quick's pawns." His lips curved in a grim smile. "But my father didn't make it out of Purgatory. He died there, and I got to see it all go down."

She shivered.

"*That's* who I am, Chloe. I'm not some safe guy that you can fool around with. Me, jealous? That's not what you want. That's not what anyone wants. Hell, I know I'm dangerous. Because I'm more like that bastard than I want to admit. What if I snap one day? What if something pushes me over the edge?" Now emotion was breaking through his voice. "I already do want you more than I should, but, baby, I am my father's son."

She stared at all of those scars. So many scars, all on the outside, easy to see.

"My scars aren't on the outside," Chloe confessed.

"Chloe?"

"He never left scars on the outside. Reporters might have seen them, and my father was far too smart to make a mistake like that."

He'd shared his past. And hadn't Connor said before...if one shared, the other would, too? Such an exchange of past pain only seemed fair.

"Donald Quick was charming. He was handsome. He always knew just the right thing to say to the right people. You looked at him, and you wanted to believe every single thing he said." Even though his words had been lies. "But who he was in public, that man wasn't anything like the guy I saw in private." A man given to screaming rages. A man consumed by the idea of power — power that would come from being a werewolf.

"My mother ran away when I was a child. She fell in love with someone else, and she just...left. But she didn't get far. For years, I believed that she'd been the victim of a hit and run, but, on my eighteenth birthday, he told me the truth. He'd killed her. Because she wanted to leave him. If I tried to leave — because then, I was so sick of his rages and the constant tests he was doing on me — he said he'd do the same thing to me. You see, no one could be allowed to humiliate the senator. No one."

And right then, Chloe made a decision. She'd already been thinking about what she would do to save Harris. And now she knew what she had to do to save herself. To keep that little bit of soul that she still had.

Everyone deserved some happiness, even if that happiness was fleeting.

Keeping her gaze on Connor, Chloe stripped off her shirt. She shed her jeans. Then she stood before him in just her bra and panties. There were no scars for him to see on her body. After his hell, the wounds to her emotions would seem like nothing.

But...

"I think you and I are more alike than you realize," she told him. "We're alike, but we are *nothing* like our fathers." Because she had made that vow to herself. To do anything necessary in order *not* to wind up being as twisted as her father had been, especially in the end. "Can I tell you a secret?"

Connor's gaze had dropped to her body. Heated. He gave a jerky nod.

"I want you." There, she'd said it. "I don't care who you were before. I don't care about any scars you have. I want you." He needed to understand that. She was the last person who'd judge him.

"You know…" His voice was more beast than man. "That I'd do anything to have you."

No, she hadn't known that. His words gave her the courage to continue.

"You asked if I'd had sex with Keegan."

His hands clenched.

"The truth is…I haven't had sex with anyone."

His head jerked up then, and he stared at her in shock.

"I wanted to, but…at sixteen, I was attacked by a pack of werewolves. They bit me, and that's when my change started. I could never control it. And when I was angry or…or aroused, the change would come out more. The last thing I

wanted to do was accidentally use my claws to
rip open a lover."

So she'd pulled away. Kept a distance
between herself and the men who'd come into
her life. Keegan…she'd never planned to go far
with him because she hadn't wanted to hurt him.

Guess he and I were both keeping secrets.

She wanted no secrets between her and
Connor. "My silver sensitivity is back. So it's
probably just a matter of time until the rest of
my…well, until everything else is back, too."
Then she'd return to the land of pain and terror.
"Before that, I want to be with you. I want to
know what it's like to go wild in a man's arms
and not fear hurting him."

Connor didn't move. "I'm not a man, baby.
You know I'm more. And I don't want to hurt
you."

She stepped toward him. Put her hand on his
chest. His skin was so warm. Almost blazing hot.
And his muscles were like stone beneath her
touch. "I don't think you ever would." Her gaze
searched his. "You have your control." She knew
that.

He shook his head. "Not with you. With you,
it breaks."

She pushed up on her toes. Skimmed her lips
over his throat. Felt the frantic beat of his pulse
beneath her mouth. "I trust you, and I want you."

She needed this. Before midnight, before the pain that would come, Chloe had to be with him.

Just once. Shouldn't she get one time? To want and be wanted?

You can still love and be loved.

Chloe slammed the door on that thought, hating the whisper that had just slipped through her mind.

She licked his skin, then lightly scored him with her teeth.

Connor shuddered against her. "You shouldn't...*I* shouldn't..."

Oh, they most certainly should. She kissed a sensual path down his chest. Carefully, she spent time pressing her lips to each scar, hating the pain that he'd endured. His father had been a true bastard, and she was glad the man was dead. Glad that he'd never hurt Connor or anyone else again.

His body seemed to grow even harder, even hotter as she kissed him. Her hands feathered over him. She loved touching Connor. He was so powerful.

Down, down she went.

"Chloe..."

Her knees hit the wooden floor. Her fingers didn't even tremble when she reached for the snap of his jeans. She popped that snap and pulled down the zipper.

He grabbed her hands.

"I want this," she said, looking up at him. "I want you." So she didn't have the practical experience, that wasn't holding her back. She'd always been a fast learner. She wasn't fighting claws and a painful change. She was riding the crest of desire she always felt when Connor was near.

"Us…what we do…it will change everything." His words sounded like a warning, but his hold had eased on her.

She wrapped her hands around his fully erect cock. So long and strong. Wider than her wrist. "I don't care." Chloe put her mouth on him. Her lips slid over the head of his arousal. Her tongue feathered over him, and then she took him deeper into her mouth, fighting to gain a rhythm even as she savored the slightly salty taste of him.

Every lick of her tongue, every move of her mouth seemed to turn Chloe on more and more. She'd thought to bring him pleasure. She hadn't realized just how wild she'd make herself. She wanted more and more and —

He lifted her up. Pretty much yanked away her bra and panties and put her on the bed. She bounced a little and heard the ragged heave of her breath.

His eyes were glittering. Connor stared at Chloe as if he could devour her right then.

Yes, please.

His hands closed over her thighs. He pulled her to the edge of the bed, opened her legs wide, and stared down at her sex. "So pretty." His voice was a growl. A deep, sensual growl that rumbled over her. "Pink and pretty." Then he put his mouth on her.

There was no hesitation from Connor. He licked her. Stroked her with his fingers and his mouth and he had Chloe arching off that bed.

But when she tried to pull away from him because it was too much, too intense, her whole body was quivering — he held her hips. He kept her against his mouth and —

She came. An explosion that burst through her body. Chloe started to scream his name because it was seriously that amazingly good.

Then she remembered where she was. Who could hear them. She bit her lower lip, bit it hard to hold back her cries as she rode out that powerful storm of release.

Connor rose slowly. Pushed his body up so that he was above her. "Was that the first?" Connor wanted to know.

She managed a nod.

"Good, fucking —" He broke off and his eyes fell on her mouth. "Oh, Chloe…you're bleeding."

She hadn't felt the pain.

"Let me help…" Then his mouth was on hers. He kissed her so softly. So carefully then…

His fingers slid over her breasts. Traced her nipples. His touch had her eagerly pushing up against him. Was the desire supposed to return so fast? She'd come, but she already wanted him again. Her nipples felt hyper-sensitive, and his every touch had her yearning to feel more...to feel him, deep inside.

He was kissing her neck now. Hot, open-mouthed kisses that seemed to send a streak of fire right to her sex. She was wet and hot for him, and she wanted Connor *inside* of her this time when she came.

"There's pleasure in the bite..." Connor's voice was such a delicious rumble. "Let me give you pleasure, Chloe."

She wanted him to give her everything. There was no going back. Chloe knew that. A few more hours, and her life would be over. She needed every bit of pleasure now. She needed Connor — *now.*

So she turned her head and she offered him her throat. A sign of submission for a wolf. For a vampire? It was an invitation.

"You give yourself to me, Chloe?"

"Yes." She wanted him *in* her. She wanted to give him all that she had and to take everything he had to give her. She would remember this moment — this time — with him, always. Because Chloe knew she would need something to hold tight when the nightmares came later. When all she had were nightmares.

She'd remember him.

His teeth raked over her throat. No, his fangs. And when his fangs sank into her, she braced for a quick flash of pain.

Pleasure.

She came right then. She shuddered and bucked beneath him but the pleasure wasn't ending. There was no crest—it just kept going and going.

His cock was at the apex of her thighs. His mouth still on her throat. His fingers slid between the folds of her sex. Connor opened her, positioned her, and he sank in deep. So deep.

She still felt no pain. With Connor, there was only pleasure.

In and out, he withdrew, then thrust. The bed rocked beneath them. Her hands grabbed frantically to his shoulders. She was maddened, driven totally wild by the pleasure.

No fear.

No pain.

Nothing but Connor and pleasure.

"You taste fucking delicious." He licked her neck. "And you feel like heaven." He drove into her, moving, if possible, even deeper. His thrusts became harder and rougher. She wanted to give him as much pleasure as he was giving to her. Wanted him to turn wild just like her.

Her legs wrapped around him. Chloe squeezed him deep inside. More, *more*.

"Everything," Connor demanded.

She looked into his eyes. Saw them glowing both with the power of a werewolf...and a vampire. His mouth came back down, but not to her neck. His lips pressed to the curve of her shoulder. He kissed her skin, right in that spot, a spot she knew was sacred to a werewolf.

A marking spot.

She started to tense, but the pleasure lashed her again. So much pleasure that she couldn't suck in a deep breath. She could only feel, caught up in a storm that wouldn't end, a climax that had her muscles quivering.

He's not marking me...that's for mates...he's not —

"Mine," she heard him say. And his teeth bit that sweet spot.

She ignited.

He came. She felt the hot jets of his release inside of her. And his mouth pressed a tender kiss to the spot he'd just marked. "Mine," again, but there was such pleasure in that word.

Pleasure and possession.

***

"Sonofabitch." Eric Pate glared at the narrow flight of stairs. He'd been intending to go up those stairs and interrogate Chloe Quick. But Connor was up there with her, and from the sound of things...the guy was doing a whole hell of a lot more than just an interrogation session.

His nostrils flared. His sense of smell was more acute than most people realized. Right then, he could smell sex. Smell blood. A terrible combination for a man like Connor.

The case had been delicate enough before. But now that Connor had screwed the pretty she-wolf, things were about to get blown to hell.

Connor wasn't going to like what they'd have to do next. It was highly doubtful that he'd have sex with a woman one moment and then — quite literally — throw her to the wolves in the next instant.

Had Chloe been counting on that?

A deal had been offered downstairs. It was a deal that they would be taking. And Chloe...hell, she was going to be the bait in his trap.

If Connor fought him on this one, Eric might just have to toss the guy into containment until the smoke cleared. The mission was about far more than just one woman. Emotions couldn't get involved.

Not when so many lives were on the line.

He straightened his shoulders. He might have to get clawed for this, but...Eric headed up the stairs.

CHAPTER SEVEN

He was afraid to look into Chloe's eyes. *A woman says it's her first time and what do I do? Literally jump on her like a starving wolf.*

He'd marked her. He hadn't meant to do that. He hadn't even meant to so much as sip her delectable blood. A vampire got too much power when he drank from a live victim. Before, he'd been desperate. If he hadn't taken her blood at the safe house, those werewolves would have taken her away from him.

This time, though...

I took her blood because I couldn't stop myself.

He'd seen the gleaming drop of blood on her lip. He'd licked it away and been lost. His control had shredded, and he'd held on just long enough to make certain she wanted the bite. Then...

"Chloe?" Connor rasped her name and pushed up on his arms. After everything else, he sure didn't want to crush her with his body.

But she just sighed and held tighter to him. Already, he was growing hard for her again.

He'd just pretty much gutted himself with pleasure, and now he already wanted her again?

She doesn't realize what I've done.

Hell, he didn't even know *why* he'd done it.

Drinking her blood…that was dangerous. Because a vampire could exert too much power over his prey. He could compel, if he wanted. He could force Chloe to do anything because he'd taken her blood. He'd tied her to him.

Any place she went now, he'd find her. He could track her, *feel* her.

Taking her blood had been bad enough, but…

He pressed a kiss to the mark he'd left on the curve of her shoulder. The vampire in him hadn't been the only one to want Chloe. His werewolf side had claimed her. He'd actually *marked* her in the way of mates.

How screwed up was that?

She'd asked for sex and he'd gone full-on primal with her—

A knock shook the door. "Get decent," Eric barked. "And then open this door."

Fury streaked through him. The last thing he wanted was to deal with Eric right then. Not when he was still buried—balls deep—in Chloe. Not when he was realizing just how tangled their web was and not when—

"Thank you," Chloe whispered. "I never knew it could be like that."

Well, that was because it usually wasn't. He'd had sex before, rushed sex, slow sex, rough sex...but nothing had ever been like that. With Chloe, everything had been different. Every sensation had been heightened. When the climax had hit him, he'd nearly howled his pleasure.

Instead, he'd claimed her.

I'm sorry, Chloe.

"I shouldn't have...done that," he told her. Hating it—hating it so much—he slowly pulled from her body. She gave a little gasp that made him want to thrust right back into her. A sexy, breathless sound.

Chloe was going to be the death of him, he just had that feeling.

"Why not?" Chloe stared up at him. "I wanted you. I still want you." Her hand lifted and pressed to his cheek.

His head turned and he kissed her palm. "You don't know what I did." Guilt was tearing through him. "Chloe, I—"

"You think I don't know a werewolf mating? Really?" She shook her head. A faint smile teased her lips. "I know." Her smile slipped. "But I also know what's coming for me. I wasn't ever meant to have one of those happily-ever-after lives. For me, those dreams ended a long time ago."

He didn't understand what she was saying.

Eric was pounding on the door again. Seriously, that SOB needed to back off.

"And your bite didn't hurt." She seemed to consider the matter a bit and added, "I think I could grow addicted to that bite."

Because that was how vampires had been designed. When they wanted it to be so, their bites could give their prey nothing but pleasure. So much pleasure that the victim would submit, again and again, to the vampire.

I don't want Chloe to be prey...or to be a victim. I just want her.

He rose from the bed. Jerked on his jeans.

Chloe rose, too. She grabbed her clothes and headed for the small bathroom. When she stumbled, he immediately grabbed her elbow. "I was too fucking rough," he muttered. "Baby, I'm sorry." If he could do it again...*would my control hold?* Because he'd never wanted anyone the way he wanted her.

When she'd kissed his scars...when she'd looked at him and actually seemed to understand him...*there is no one like Chloe.*

And he was in way over his head.

"You were exactly what I wanted," Chloe said.

"*Open the damn door!*" Eric yelled.

Connor snarled back at him.

"You think I'm scared of your wolf?" Eric shouted as he pounded on the door again. "Try that again! I will send your ass back to Purgatory as fast as you can blink. I know what you've done in there! I told you — *hands off!* Did you listen? Oh, hell no, you didn't."

Eric was ranting. Figured.

"I'm all right," Chloe said. "Just, give me a minute, okay?"

He hated to do it, but Connor let her go. He watched as she headed into the bathroom. Chloe closed the door. The soft click seemed a little too loud.

He stared at that closed bathroom door. Then, squaring his shoulders, he headed toward Eric. Before Eric could pound again, Connor yanked the room's door open. "You are pissing me off," Connor told him.

Eric lifted a brow. "So sorry to interrupt your fucking fun time with the little —"

Something snapped in Connor. He grabbed Eric — his *boss* — and shoved him back out of the room. His claws burst from his fingertips as he rammed Eric into the nearest wall.

"*She-wolf!*" Eric yelled. "Hell, man, all I was going to say was *little she-wolf!*"

Connor tried to choke back his rage, and, after about ten seconds, he managed to let go of Eric.

"Why do I put up with this shit?" Eric muttered. "I should slap a silver collar on you and just be done."

"The collar won't work. You know that. The silver does nothing to me. Not since you made me into—"

"A paranormal super soldier?" Eric straightened his shirt. "That's right, I did. You're welcome for that."

He thought about biting the guy, just for spite.

"You drank her blood." Eric glanced toward the room behind Connor. "That could work to our advantage. We need to infiltrate this pack, so I'll get you to compel Chloe to go in for us and to—"

He lunged for the guy again. But, Eric, showing strength he shouldn't have, caught Connor around the neck and held him back.

"I get that you're angry because I interrupted at the not-so-best time," Eric muttered. "So I gave you one attack. I don't have time to shit away with another."

Connor's claws were inches from Eric's face. Just what kind of damage would they do to each other if they fought?

"Compel Chloe, and let's get a team ready to go. You having her blood makes things easier. At least now I know we can trust her."

Eric still had a hand on Connor's throat, and Connor's claws were poised to rip into Eric. "I'm not compelling her."

For the first time ever, Connor saw surprise flash on Eric's face. "What? Why the hell not?"

The door creaked behind him. "Because he doesn't need to," Chloe said. "I'm going to make the trade. I'll get Harris back for you, I promise."

Eric's hand slid away from Connor's throat. "Well, that was sure easier than I expected."

There was a dull pounding in Connor's ears. He turned to face Chloe. She stood in that doorway, looking even more delicate and fragile than before. Her hair was loose, pulled forward around her neck and shoulders. *To hide my mark?* She was dressed in her jeans and t-shirt. And her face...her cheeks were still flushed. Her lips red. She was so beautiful to him that he couldn't look away from her.

"I planned to do the trade all along. Ever since I saw the video."

Now he knew why she'd wanted to make love with him. Chloe thought she was heading out on some kind of suicide mission. "It's not happening."

She shook her head. "I can't let him die."

"And I *won't* let you die." Didn't she get that she was important to him?

Then he realized...no, she didn't. Because Chloe was right. He'd been little more than a jailer to her. And it wasn't like Connor was big on sharing his feelings. Hell, he hadn't thought he was capable of actually caring for a woman, until her.

Everything was changing for him.

Eric clapped his hands together. "Great. Fantastic. Seems like everything is settled."

Nothing was settled. Eric was insane.

Eric pointed to Chloe. "Come downstairs and we'll see if we can find you some easy-to-conceal weapons. Unfortunately, silver will burn you as much as it burns them, but maybe I've got some other gadgets we can use."

Eric turned away.

"Nothing is settled," Connor said, each word snapping out. "She's not trading herself."

Chloe smiled at Connor. "I wasn't asking for permission from you. Like I said, this is what I planned to do all along." Then she slid right past him.

Connor shook his head. "I just want you safe—"

"And that's why you'll be going into Eclipse with her." Eric spoke as if Connor should have already figured that part out. "I mean, come on…it's a werewolf bar. You're a werewolf. Partly, anyway. You'll blend perfectly."

Yeah, there was one thing Eric seemed to be missing… "*She* won't. The instant the other wolves smell her, what do you think they'll do?"

Eric's grin stretched. "See, that's where you come into the equation. If they launch at her, you'll be there. It's such a handy thing you're good at kicking ass."

***

"I didn't even know this place existed," Chloe said as she stared out the passenger window of the SUV and her gaze raked the exterior of Eclipse. From the outside, Eclipse looked just like any other run-down bar. But Eric had told her that it was actually a werewolf hangout. Humans never got past the doors, and she could certainly see why. Two big men—scary, guys who were as wide as they were thick—stood guarding the doors. Bouncers to the extreme.

"I thought you were all worried about her scent."

This came was from the other guy who'd accompanied their little party. Agent Duncan McGuire. She turned her head and found him frowning at her. The dude had just sniffed her. "I don't smell anything different about her."

"That's because you're like Connor, half vamp, half wolf," Eric said. "I was a little nervous earlier when we were watching the video, but you didn't so much as twitch when you were near her." He paused, then added, "Besides, you're mated to Holly...and nothing trumps a werewolf mating. So even if you hadn't been all vamped up, well, that probably means you wouldn't be influenced by Chloe's scent."

He was mated to Holly? The vampire doctor? The pieces snapped together for her. "Wait! You're Connor's brother?"

Duncan glanced toward the front of the SUV. Connor was in passenger seat up there. "Guilty."

"So…you're the one he wanted to kill?" Only now they were both working at the Para Unit? Oh, there was so much more to the story that she needed to hear.

Duncan was still staring up at Connor. "I see you've been talking about me."

Connor grunted. "This plan is shit."

Ah, so obviously he wasn't in the mood to share about his family. And maybe this wasn't the best time. She had five minutes to go until midnight, so her fear level was about to shoot through the roof.

"The fact that her scent doesn't influence Duncan is a good thing," Eric pointed out. The guy sure seemed oddly calm. Did he have ice water in his veins or what? "It means Duncan can go in and provide back-up for you two without us having to worry he'll go crazy."

"I'd prefer for no one to go crazy," Chloe said, just so they were all clear.

"Too late," was Eric's instant reply. "It sure looks like Keegan has gone over the line."

She glanced back at the entrance to Eclipse. "What if those guys don't let Connor and Duncan go inside with me?"

"Oh, they'll let us in…" Connor's voice was certain. "We're not giving them a choice."

Then he opened his door. Crap, that open door meant it was show time. Or, rather, trade time.

She started to push open her door.

Eric grabbed her arm. He was in the driver's seat—fitting, since he was in charge of this plan—and he'd leaned back to grab her before she could slip out. "Remember, wherever you go, Connor can find you. He has your blood, and that's all he needs. Even if the pack takes you away from here, we'll come for you."

His words were supposed to be reassuring. They weren't. Because what if Keegan didn't plan to take her anyplace? What if he planned to kill her on sight?

That was her fear. Her worst, horrible fear. And it was the reason she'd wanted to be with Connor so badly. To have one good, perfect moment to remember. Pleasure, to fight the pain.

Part of her just wanted to turn and run. But she couldn't do that. If she didn't go in that bar, Harris Grey would die.

Connor opened her door. Eric's fingers slid away from her arm. Connor reached for her hand. She put her fingers in his.

She stepped from the SUV. Stood at Connor's side. Duncan had already climbed from the vehicle, too. They waited there, just a moment.

"You don't have to do this," Connor told her, voice rough.

"Yes, I do."

The lights were blazing in Eclipse, but she heard no noise. No music. No laughter. In a werewolf bar, she should have heard those sounds, right?

They started walking.

Eric hadn't wanted to just storm the place because he'd said that if he did, Harris would likely be killed immediately.

So he'd agreed to Keegan's rules, up to a point.

With every step that she took, Chloe felt her fear mounting. She wanted to be strong. She wanted to face Keegan without a tremble shaking her body. She wanted—

Her claws were coming out.

She looked down at her hands and saw the claws there.

"And your eyes are glowing," Connor told her softly. "You're beautiful."

The two bouncers saw them coming. Their faces twisted as they looked at Connor and Duncan.

"I told you," Chloe said, "they aren't going to let you two in!"

One of the bouncers lunged for Connor. Connor broke away from Chloe. He grabbed the bouncer and tossed the guy a good ten feet. When the man hit the ground, he hit with a very hard thud.

"My turn," Duncan muttered. The other guard was charging at him. Running fast and—

Duncan shot him.

Smoke rose from the man's stomach as he fell.

"Silver always wins. Doesn't matter the werewolf's size," Duncan said.

Right. The two bouncers—wounded now— were staying down.

Duncan opened the door to Eclipse. Connor went in first. Chloe sucked in a quick breath, and she followed right behind him. Duncan was pulling up the rear, and she didn't look back, but she strongly suspected he had his gun at the ready.

Eclipse was so bright inside. Every light was on, so it was easy to see Harris Grey. He was in the middle of the room, bound and gagged and bleeding. His eyes were terrified as he stared at them, and he muttered frantically behind the gag.

"I can smell them," Connor said, "their scents are all over this place."

But no wolves were actually there. At least, not any she saw.

Chloe hurried toward Harris. Her fingers fumbled as she reached for his gag.

"No!" Harris yelled. "Get out! It's a trap!"

Chloe shook her head. "It's a trade. Me, for you." She yanked at his ropes and her claws cut right through them. Well, at least her claws were coming in handy.

There was so much blood on Harris, and the man was deathly pale. She pulled him to his feet. "Go out the door. Eric is waiting in the SUV."

But Harris didn't move. "He...bit me."

Oh, hell. A werewolf bite would mean either transformation or death.

Duncan grabbed the guy and shoved Harris toward the door. "Get to Pate, get to him *now*."

***

Keegan James stared at the bar. His hands were clenched into fists, and his claws cut deeply into his palms.

He'd kept the pack away, because he hadn't wanted them to go wild when they caught Chloe's scent. He'd intended to go in Eclipse for her. He had snipers set up to take out the two Para Agents who'd gone in with her but...

Something is different with Chloe.

Her scent had changed. It didn't lure him now. Didn't tempt and torment.

Because she was fucking *mated.*

He lifted his phone. The order would be given to all. "Kill every single one of them. They don't get out alive. *None* of them."

He strode from the shadows and headed toward Eclipse. He would handle Chloe personally.

Once, he'd had such fine plans for her. Now, she was fucking useless to him.

So he might as well kill her.

She'll see...no one betrays me and lives. No one.

***

Chloe looked around the bar. She still didn't see any of the werewolves. There were long claw marks on the walls, on the floor. But where were Keegan and his pack?

Then she heard the howls. They were coming from outside. A wild chorus that was getting...louder? Closer?

"Am I supposed to stay here?" Chloe asked, her heart racing. "You guys take Harris and they take me?" Because from the sound of those howls, the pack was closing in—fast.

Connor shook his head. "That isn't how this will work."

The howls were louder. She flinched. Harris had gone outside and Duncan had run out, too. Probably to make sure Harris didn't get eaten on his way to safety.

She lunged forward because she needed to make sure they were both okay.

Glass exploded from the window to her right. A fully shifted werewolf had just leapt through that window and sent glass raining down on her.

Another wolf burst through the window to the left.

Those two wolves lunged at Connor, their mouths snapping as saliva dripped from their fangs.

"Connor!"

He drove his fist right at one charging werewolf. The other sank its teeth into Connor's leg.

She ran toward him—

"No, you don't get to help him." A hard hand grabbed Chloe and yanked her back.

That voice. Chloe knew that voice. Her head turned and she stared into Keegan's glowing eyes.

"I had such fine plans for you, but you went and screwed that up...by *screwing* him."

More werewolves were rushing inside. Several had surrounded Connor. He was fighting them, swiping out with his claws even as they leapt at him.

"Did you think I wouldn't know?" Keegan pulled her even closer against him. "I can smell him on you."

"Keegan..."

"That scent trick of your father's isn't working anymore. I can see you for the useless wolf you are."

Chloe shook her head.

"Smart of him," Keegan continued, voice almost thoughtful. "He must have done it to try and attract a powerful mate for you. Guess he thought an alpha's blood would carry down to any children you had."

"*Chloe!*" Connor roared her name.

She risked another glance at him. Four werewolves were on the ground near him and Connor was turning toward her, but two more wolves had just jumped on him.

"But you picked the wrong alpha, sweetheart." Keegan's hands lifted and locked around her neck.

Is he going to strangle me?

She struggled against him. Clawed him, kicked him, fought—

"You should have picked me."

Then he just…snapped her neck.

CHAPTER EIGHT

"Chloe!"

He heard the snap, a soft crack, as the dark-haired bastard broke Chloe's neck.

Connor threw the wolves off him and leapt toward Chloe. She was falling—Keegan had just dropped her, and Connor grabbed Chloe before she could hit the ground.

"Too late, asshole," Keegan snarled.

Connor didn't look up at him. He couldn't take his eyes off Chloe. She was so still. Her head slumped to the side. "Chloe, baby, open your eyes!"

"Hard to do…" That fucking bastard said, "when she's dead."

Connor put his hand on Chloe's throat, desperately trying to find a pulse. But there wasn't one. No pulse and she wasn't breathing.

"I snapped too hard, hmmm? She always was too weak."

A shifted werewolf slammed into Connor's back. He felt teeth tear into his shoulder.

"Kill him," Keegan ordered. "Let him join the slut in death."

Connor heard the growls. The howls. The other werewolves were closing in on him.

Connor's head lifted. His gaze met Keegan's.

Keegan smiled. "Aw, did I just kill the bitch you'd taken for a mate? My bad."

"I am going to hurt you so fucking much," Connor promised him. "By the time I am done, you will be begging me to end you." *She can't be gone. She can't be gone.*

Fury and fear exploded within him, spiraling out of control. His claws and fangs were fully extended. Rage ripped through him, and Connor felt his bones begin to snap.

She can't be gone.

He lowered her to the floor, touched her hair. His hands were still those of a man, even though he had claws.

He could hear thunder in the distance. So much thunder.

Gunshots?

The wolves were swiping at him. He didn't feel pain. His rage was too strong.

I will kill them all. Every single fucking one.

Chloe's eyes were closed. Her heart wasn't beating.

And Keegan was still laughing.

Connor swiped out at the wolf nearest him. He caught the bastard in the throat. Blood flowed.

I will kill them all.

His bones were popping. Fur burst along his arms. His hands slammed onto the floor — but, they were changing, too. He had paws. His spine reshaped, he transformed —

Bam! Bam! Bam!

The wolves around him fell back and the scent of burning flesh and silver filled the air.

"Shit, he's shifting!" That was Duncan's voice. And when he looked up, he saw Duncan in that doorway, right beside Eric. Both men held guns in each of their hands, and they were firing, again and again.

The wolves weren't stopping though. One jumped onto Eric and took the man down. They crashed onto the floor.

Two more lunged at Duncan. He shot one and the other attacked with his mouth open. "I don't think so," Duncan muttered. "Been there, done that bite shit before." He kicked out and the werewolf flew back against the wall.

Destroy. Kill. Connor's thoughts were becoming more primal as he shifted. Chloe was on the floor, her eyes closed, her body chillingly still. It shouldn't have been that way for her. He'd promised to protect her.

Grief tore through him and pumped up his rage and hate to killing levels. All control was gone. It was—

Her eyes opened.

The world stopped for him right then. Chloe's stare met his. Her eyes were so big, so blue, so *alive.*

He knew she'd been dead just seconds before. But Chloe was rising, pushing herself up. Her hair slid over her cheek as she slowly turned her head. Her neck popped a bit, as if the bones had slid back into place.

She came back to me!

His wolf howled.

"What the fuck?" Keegan shouted. "How in the hell are you still alive?"

Kill. Connor flew at the man. He took him down, slamming Keegan onto the floor. He went in ready to rip the guy's throat right out, but Keegan threw him off and jumped right back to his feet.

"Fool!" Keegan glared at him. "You think you're the only one who can drink vamp blood and become something more?" He flashed fangs. "Yeah, I know what you are. I realized it the other night. Now let's see which alpha is stronger."

"C-Connor?"

His head whipped to the right. Chloe was on her feet. She looked lost, confused. She rubbed her neck and glanced around the chaos in Eclipse. The scene was filled with fighting wolves and blood. "Connor!"

He realized that she didn't know he was a wolf. She was searching for him, moving so slowly and seeming confused by everything around her. Everything and everyone.

Because she was dead before.

"This is interesting," Keegan said. "Maybe there are more surprises from my Chloe." His eyes glinted. "I just have to make sure I kill the bastard who mated her first." He moved in a blur, running right for Connor and he swiped his razor sharp claws along Connor's back.

Connor was distracted—still looking at Chloe—and he turned back to Keegan too late.

The bastard laughed as he retreated. "First blood's mine. Ready to see what a real alpha can do?"

But right then, another wolf slammed into Chloe. She screamed and then her arm flew out. Connor knew the wolf was going to bite her. Connor's hind legs pushed down, and he surged across the room, focused only on getting to her.

But Chloe grabbed the wolf around the neck. "No." Connor heard her soft voice so clearly.

Then she just tossed that wolf aside as if he weighed nothing. With one hand.

What?

More gunfire thundered and—

"Get her the hell out of here, Duncan!" That was Eric's voice, barking a command.

Connor stood in front of Chloe.

She shuddered and looked down at him. Did she even know it was him? He needed to shift back to his human form, but if he did, he'd be vulnerable for attack.

Chloe looked at her hands, then at him. "What did I do?" She backed up, then focused on him again. "Connor?" She stared down at his wolf, and he knew right then that she saw him.

He pushed against her legs.

"I don't want to hurt you," she whispered. "Something is wrong. I-I don't think...I can't seem to control myself. I have this need..." Her whole body shook. "I want to kill."

He was one hundred percent sure the woman had just risen from the dead. She was shaking and too pale and he wanted to get her back to Holly's lab ASAP.

"Please help me," Chloe begged.

He looked across the bar. Keegan had vanished. The other wolves were fleeing through the windows. Probably because Eric was shooting silver in a frenzy.

Connor let the fire of the shift sweep through him. Hot, consuming, and his bones began to reshape.

"*Now I get to kill you...*"

Keegan's voice.

Connor's head snapped up. Keegan was just steps away, but Connor hadn't scented the bastard. He'd thought the guy had cut and run from Eclipse.

Now Keegan's claws were coming right for his head.

Gunfire rang out. A blossom of red appeared on Keegan's chest. He looked down… "Dammit!" Keegan shouted and he stumbled back.

Duncan, his gun still at the ready, rushed forward. "You don't get to kill my brother, asshole!"

Keegan scrambled away, moving fast for an injured bastard.

For just an instant, Connor remembered another time, another place. So long ago. Another attack with wolves and blood. He'd been a child, begging for his brother.

But his father had been there. That sick, twisted jerk had taken Connor away while he'd cried out for his brother

Duncan took up a protective stance in front of Connor. "Finish the shift, and let's get out of here. Those wolves could be going for reinforcements."

Connor's back bowed as the final surge of the transition swept over him. When it ended — that hard, burning agony — his hands were slapped against the floor. He was naked and back in human form.

He looked up. Chloe was staring at him. What did she see? The monster?

He rose to his feet.

Chloe wrapped her arms around him and held tight. Her whole body was trembling. "Something is wrong with me..." Chloe said again. "The fire...I can feel the fire everywhere."

And she was hot to the touch. She'd been ice cold when she was on the floor. When she lay there, her neck twisted, a broken doll because of Keegan's attack.

Connor lifted her into his arms. Eric ran out ahead and Duncan covered their backs while they left that bar.

Harris wasn't out in the SUV. Connor knew that a back-up team had been waiting in the wings. Their mission had been to get Harris to safety.

Now Connor's only goal was to get Chloe the hell out of there. Eric jumped in the front seat, Duncan rode shot-gun, and Connor climbed into the back, holding Chloe close.

She died. She died.

But she'd come back.

Eric gunned the SUV, and it lurched forward. They were hauling ass, and Connor looked back, trying to see if the werewolves were following them.

He didn't see them. Didn't smell them—Eric had left the windows open, probably thinking that Connor or Duncan would sense a tail on them.

"What's wrong with me?"

He looked down at Chloe.

"What happened in there? Why…why do I feel so strange?"

Connor didn't know what to say. His gaze jerked to the front of the SUV. He caught Eric's stare in the rear-view mirror. Eric shook his head.

Screw that. *I won't lie to her. Not to Chloe. Not anymore.*

He pulled her closer. Buried his face in the curve of her shoulder. Her arms were around him, holding tight. Her sweet scent flooded him, reassured him.

"Tell me…what happened…"

His hold hardened on her. "Baby, you died."

***

Everything seemed too loud. Too bright. And Chloe felt far too hot, as if she were burning from the inside. Eric had taken them back to the base, but only after he'd driven what felt like hell-of-forever. She knew he'd been trying to ditch anyone on their trail, but had he succeeded in losing a pack of werewolves? Was that even possible?

When he'd gone over the mission plan, Eric had said he was sending in a small group of agents to lower the risk that they'd be followed back to base. But then, she knew he'd also planned for a *successful* mission. One that had him returning triumphant.

He didn't look triumphant.

Eric was pacing in front of her. Connor—now wearing jeans and a t-shirt that stretched across his chest—was at Chloe's side.

I died? Again?

"We need Olivia in here," Connor said, his face and voice grim. "She's the one who did this—whatever the hell it is."

Chloe flinched at Olivia's name. Once upon a time, Olivia Maddox had been her best friend. As kids, they'd been inseparable. Then their lives had been shattered. At sixteen, they'd been attacked by a pack of wolves. Those wolves had been after Olivia, and Chloe had tried so hard to protect her friend.

But she hadn't been strong enough. So she'd been bitten, again and again.

Then the real nightmare had begun.

Olivia had been bitten as well, only she hadn't transformed, and she hadn't died. Olivia had healed instantly. Chloe's father had discovered that Olivia was actually someone quite unique, a djinn. A real, modern-day genie, and he'd made it his mission to take her power.

By any means necessary.

"Olivia is on her way," Holly said as she took another blood sample from Chloe. Chloe held herself completely still as the needle went into her vein. "But she's...different now, so I don't know how much help she'll be."

Chloe hadn't seen Olivia in weeks, not since that last, fateful encounter.

When my father killed me, Olivia brought me back...and then I murdered dear old dad in an act that I can't even remember!

"Her heart rate is elevated, and her body temperature is a bit higher than normal," Holly said as she stepped back from Chloe. "But otherwise, everything is normal. She doesn't even appear to have her silver sensitivity any longer."

Chloe swallowed. "That's the way it was last time." Because she'd lived this scene—well, almost this scene—before. The first time she'd died, she'd found herself in Holly's lab, undergoing test after test after test.

Holly's head tilted to the side. "Since the silver sensitivity came back before, we can only assume it will return again. Maybe your body goes through some sort of stabilization period...?"

Connor cleared his throat. "You need to check her strength."

"My what?" Chloe asked.

Connor shook his head. "Your strength, baby. Because I saw you pick up a werewolf and toss him across the room as if he were no heavier than a pillow. I can do that, Duncan can—but you already know where our power comes from."

Super wolf. Super vamp. She nodded, but rubbed her neck. It ached a bit. "I don't…remember doing that." Her hand dropped. "I just remember looking for you." At first, she'd been looking for him as a man. She'd only seen wolves though. Then she'd looked into the eyes of a big, powerful wolf…and she'd seen Connor. His golden gaze had stared back at her.

"Dies…and comes back." Eric stopped pacing and glared at Chloe. "You aren't supposed to do that."

She glared back at him. "Sorry. Guess I missed the memo on that."

He pulled out his gun.

Chloe jumped off that exam table and Connor immediately stepped in front of her.

"What in the hell are you doing?" Connor demanded.

She peaked around his body and saw Eric contemplating his gun. "Holly should see what occurs when she dies and comes back. Then we might be able to figure out what's really happening."

Connor leapt forward and yanked the gun out of Eric's hands. "We don't have any guarantee that she *will* come back again! You shoot her, and that could be it. She'd be gone."

His voice lowered and it sounded as if he muttered, "Then you'd be gone, too."

Chloe wrapped her arms around her stomach. "I think you're all wrong. I-I didn't die." She laughed then, and the sound was hollow even to her own ears. "Keegan must have knocked me out for a few minutes, that's all. I probably hit my head when I fell — because I was on the floor — and that's why things are a little sketchy in my memory."

Silence.

And in the face of that silence, Chloe just kept right on talking. "I don't think…maybe my father didn't kill me, either." Her words were coming too fast. "He was my father, after all…he probably missed my heart." Okay, that came out desperate. "I healed. Werewolves heal faster, right? I healed and that's all that happened that time, too."

Connor turned back to look at her. Everyone there was just looking at her.

Chloe tucked her hair behind her ear. "What? That's what happened. I didn't die. I know I didn't."

Connor stepped toward her. He caught her hands and held them in his warm grip. "I was watching you. I saw the bastard break your neck. I heard the snap."

She jerked, but he held her fast.

"You were falling, and I caught you before you hit the floor. Your heart wasn't beating. You weren't breathing."

Chloe shook her head.

"You *know* it's true, baby. You just don't want to admit it."

She needed to get away from them. "I-I need some air."

His hold just tightened on her. "You have nightmares every night, don't you? But are those nightmares about your father? Or are they about you dying?"

Her eyes were filling with tears. "Stop." She didn't want to hear any more right then.

"You talk about fire..."

"Stop!" She could feel the flames on her skin.

"Where do you go...when you die, Chloe?"

"I don't die!"

The door to the lab opened. Olivia stood there. Her hair had been pulled into a long braid—a familiar sight to Chloe—and Olivia's eyes were filled with sorrow as she stared at Chloe. "I'm sorry."

Chloe shook her head. "You don't need to be. My father—he's the one who set all of this in motion. He hunted you—"

"You were bitten because you were protecting me." Olivia strode toward her. "You were trying to save me, and it cost you everything."

It hurt to look at Olivia. Her father had done so much to cause her friend pain.

"Chloe. Please."

She forced herself to meet Olivia's stare.

"I did this to you." Olivia's lips trembled. "He killed you, and I-I didn't even stop to think. I just wished."

Chloe's breath was coming faster. Her chest hurt because her heart was pounding too hard.

"I made the wish. I wished you'd be alive, and you came back. You were alive."

She had to get out of there. They were all staring at her with pity and confusion in their gazes. Chloe rushed around Olivia and ran for the door.

But another man was there. One who'd entered with Olivia. Big, blond, and blocking her exit.

"I can't let you go," he said, voice soft. "None of us can."

She looked back at Olivia. Her friend's shoulders had sagged. "That wasn't the only wish I made," Olivia said.

"Stop!" Chloe didn't want to hear any more. She didn't want to hear that she was now some kind of undead freak. Her life was more than screwed up enough as it was. Frantic now, her gaze locked on Connor. He would help her. Connor always helped her. "Get me out of here, please."

Connor walked toward her.

Her breath came a little easier.

But then he shook his head.

No. "Connor?"

"You *died,*" he said, "and that gutted me."

She could only stare at him.

"We need to know exactly what we're dealing with here." He glanced over at Olivia. "So tell me what else you wished."

Olivia's hands clenched at her sides. "I didn't realize how...how the wishes would work. I'd been told that they came out darker, that you never really got the exact thing that you wanted..."

Because, according to legend, the djinn had been creatures of darkness. They took wishes, twisted them, and...well, her father had said they grew stronger with every dark wish they granted.

"I thought I had to say the wishes in order for them to come true," Olivia continued. Her words were husky. Sad. "Later, I realized..." Her words trailed away.

Eric sighed. "All right, let's hurry this along." He waved his hand. "She just had to think the wishes. If she thought them, bam, they came true."

Miserably, Olivia nodded. "I wished for you to be alive, but then...I was making another wish." She looked over at the big, blond male — the one still blocking the exit. "Shane stopped me

before I could say it, but it was still in my head."
Her shoulders sagged. "I'm sorry."

She shouldn't ask. She shouldn't. "What were you wishing?"

"I *did* wish it." Olivia crept toward her. She took Chloe's hand and held tight. "You are my best friend, Chloe. You were dying in front of me. No, you were dead. I didn't think. I just wished."

Chloe couldn't breathe.

"I wished for you to be alive." Olivia nervously wet her lips. "And the wish I didn't get to voice, the one only in my mind…"

Just say it!

"I wished that you'd come back. That you'd never die."

Chloe took a step back.

Olivia's hold tightened on her. "I didn't know it would mean you could be killed — that you'd die and come back in some kind of endless cycle! I didn't know! I just wanted to help you!" Tears filled her eyes. "I'm sorry! I'm so sorry!"

"Wh-what am I?" Chloe asked. "Am I a zombie?" Like in a horror show? Was she going to go crazy and start eating brains?

"No!" That fast response came from Holly. "Your heart is beating, your brain is functioning. You're very much alive."

"But I can't…die?"

"No, you die," Connor said grimly. The faint lines on his face appeared deeper. "I saw you. You were gone."

"I just don't stay gone?" Her head was throbbing. Her whole body shaking. "Where do I go?"

No one spoke. Chloe's gaze flew from one of them to another.

And her terror just got worse.

***

Chloe had been holding out on him. She wasn't just a werewolf. She was something far, far more important.

Chloe could cheat death. Die, then come back, better than before.

Keegan kept his gaze on the nondescript building. He could see the men patrolling the building's perimeter — acting as if they were just security guards. But security guards weren't usually equipped with that much fire power.

He'd tracked them back to this base. With the way the men had been bleeding, it had been like child's play. *And…just in case we had lost them…I took the liberty of stacking the odds in my favor.*

He doubted they'd even found the little tracking device that he'd shoved into one of Harris's wounds.

"What now, alpha?"

He smiled. "Now we just wait for our moment to attack." Because he had an end game of his own. Originally, many of his men had gone to Purgatory because they'd been following the orders of David Vincent. Vincent and the senator had thought their plans were so fucking perfect.

They hadn't been.

Now Keegan needed his men back. He wanted them out of Purgatory, and the only way that would happen...*I need those Para Agents to release them.*

One way or another, he'd be getting his werewolves.

Even if he had to take a little trip to Purgatory in order to make that happen.

CHAPTER NINE

"Unwish it."

Chloe's shaking voice broke Connor's heart.

"I-I shouldn't be like this. No one should die and come back." Chloe's face was far too pale as she stared at Olivia. "Just unwish it. Put me back the way I was before."

Connor already knew that couldn't happen, even before Olivia shook her head.

"Please," Chloe said.

"She can't," Connor said as he wrapped his arm around Chloe. He needed to get her alone. She was so close to breaking, he could see it. And he didn't want her around everyone else when she was hurting so much. He wanted to take her out of there and just hold her. "Olivia isn't a djinn anymore. Shane changed her. She's a vamp."

And after that change, Eric had seemed confident—fairly so, anyway—that her djinn powers were gone. A good thing because, otherwise, Eric would have needed to permanently contain Olivia. A being who could kill just with a thought? There would have been no way the government could have allowed her to run around loose. She would have been far too dangerous.

"Look, everybody…" Duncan's loud voice caught his attention. "This isn't such a bad thing. We've got an indestructible woman. There are plenty of people out there who *wish* they could bounce back from any injury." Duncan slanted a glance at Eric. "I'm betting you could use a few others folks like her on your team."

Eric didn't reply.

Knowing the sneaky SOB, yeah, he probably did want more folks like Chloe. And all those tests that Holly had been running…Connor would bet that Eric was hoping Holly would find something in Chloe's blood work or in her DNA that would let the doctor replicate the condition on some federal volunteers.

"I need to go check on Harris," Eric said, giving them all a curt nod. "Connor, I trust you'll make sure that Chloe doesn't leave the facility?"

"But—" Chloe began.

"Under the circumstances, I'm sure you'll agree that you're far safer here with us," Eric said smoothly. "After all, it seems there's a pack out there that wants you dead. Since you keep rising, how many times do you think they'd kill you before they got the clue that you weren't exactly the type to stay in a grave?"

She blanched.

"Exactly. Connor, keep her here. Holly, please let me know immediately if you find out anything in her blood work and Olivia…"

Olivia glanced over at him.

"To play things safe, let's keep up your current order protocol, shall we? Don't make any wishes, don't even think them. I don't want to tempt fate." He inclined his head toward Duncan. "Follow me for a briefing." His gaze cut to Shane. "You, too."

Shane's brows lifted. "You know I don't really work for you anymore."

"Hell, you never did. But I need a favor, and if you can help, I'll owe you."

Now Shane looked intrigued.

But Connor just felt worried. He knew Eric was already cooking up some new plan, and whatever that plan was—it wouldn't be good and it wouldn't be safe. Eric's plans never were.

"I need to go outside," Chloe said as she tugged him toward the door. "I can't breathe in here."

Like he was going to deny her anything. "I know a place." There was a small, enclosed courtyard in the middle of the facility. Eric actually used that courtyard when he was interrogating vampires. A little sunlight could go a long way.

But it was night then, and the darkness…the glittering stars…they could be just what Chloe needed.

He was at the door when Eric spoke again. "Don't let her out of your sight."

Connor glanced back at him.

"This thing isn't over," Eric told him quietly. "Those wolves aren't stopping, not until *we* stop them."

"More for Purgatory?" Connor hated that place. Mostly because he'd nearly died there.

"Purgatory isn't the answer," Eric muttered. "It's the damn problem."

***

Eric braced himself before he went into the next exam room. Harris Grey was strapped to the table, and a glowing silver collar was locked around his neck.

When he heard Eric's approaching footsteps, Harris's head snapped to the left and he locked his gaze on his boss.

There was desperation in Harris's stare. Fear. Fury.

"Kill me," Harris said.

Eric shook his head. "You're not the first agent who's been bit. Death isn't the solution."

Sweat soaked Harris's body. "If I…don't change…I'll die anyway."

A most painful death.

"You have the DNA that will allow you to change. You can survive this." He'd learned a lot since taking over the Para Unit. Some good things, some bad.

The door opened behind him. He didn't look back. He knew it was Duncan McGuire. After all, he'd ordered the man to come in. Duncan had always been a good agent.

A better man.

That's why I let the lucky bastard stay with my sister. I knew he'd die for her.

Especially after what had gone down in Purgatory…yes, Duncan was a man worthy of Holly.

"I don't want…to hurt anyone…" Harris whispered. "Saw what…wolves do…"

Eric shook his head. "You saw what some wolves do. They aren't all like that. Werewolves are just like humans." A lesson he'd learned. "Some are good, some are evil." He stared into Harris's eyes, needing the guy to understand this message. "You aren't evil. You never have been, and I don't think you ever will be."

Harris's body shuddered. "I'm…scared."

Duncan stepped to Eric's side. "You should be. I won't lie to you, this isn't going to be easy and it sure won't be pretty, but you can survive it. You *will* survive it."

"The first full moon will be the hardest," Eric said. Unfortunately, the full moon would be coming soon. "Get through that, and you're good."

And if he didn't...if his beast took over and the guy went feral, then Eric would deal with him. But Eric would not take out this agent without giving Harris a fighting chance.

"I've been where you are," Duncan said to Harris. "There's a choice other than death."

But Duncan had been an alpha, and Harris...Eric didn't know how much fight the guy had in him. He'd been one tough cop in Atlanta, and he'd transferred, aiming hard and fast to move into the FBI and up the ladder there. The guy had popped up on the Para Unit's radar because his parents had been killed by supernaturals, and...well, he'd seemed properly motivated to join the group.

Now they would wait and see. Either Harris's human side would win this battle, and he'd keep the baser instincts of the werewolf in check...

Or I'll have to put him down.

***

Connor typed in a code and opened the heavy, metal door. It squeaked on its hinges as it swung out, and Chloe saw the glitter of stars. She hurried outside, but stopped short. The entire area — Connor had called it a courtyard — was enclosed in a large fence. A fence made out of what looked like —

"Silver," Connor said. "So, just to be on the safe side, don't touch it, baby."

She walked to the middle of that area. Tilted her head back and stared up at the sky. The moon was up there. Big and bright, but not quite full. Not yet.

"The full moon is close," Connor murmured. "You know that's bad for a werewolf."

Because the beast inside got stronger then.

"You scared the hell out of me."

She glanced over at Connor. His gaze wasn't on the stars or the moon. It was totally on her.

"I thought I'd lost you." He closed the distance between them. Reached out to touch her, but then stopped. "I was terrified."

Chloe shook her head. "No, not you, you don't fear anything."

"I can't lose you." Then he leaned forward. He pressed a light kiss to the curve of her neck.

Her heart gave a little jump.

"I've lost too much in my life. Some things I can't ever get back." He kissed her neck again. "I don't want to lose you." He eased back and stared into her eyes. "I'm not your jailer, Chloe. I'm here, with you now, because I want to do everything within my power to keep you safe."

"Connor—"

"It felt like my heart had been ripped out," he confessed gruffly. "And, baby, I didn't even know I still had one. Figured I'd lost it years ago when my old man was cutting into me."

Her gaze searched his.

"You got to me, Chloe," he said. "You're making me feel things that I shouldn't."

Her lips pressed together, then she made a confession of her own, saying, "I've wanted you from the beginning." But she shook her head. What she felt for Connor was more than just desire. So much more, and she didn't fully understand it. Or him. "What's happening between us?"

"Do you know how mating works for werewolves?"

She shook her head. Not really. She knew where the mating bite was given, but…not much else.

"We can mate with those who are a match for us. Genetically. Physically. We can scent the connection there, and we know that we can have children with potential mates."

Children? No, she couldn't think that far ahead. She couldn't—

"I've never wanted to mate with anyone before. When I was with you, I couldn't stop myself from marking you. *I* did that, and I should've had control. I should've held back."

"It was just a bite." She said the words to convince herself. And him.

He shook his head. "It's more, and you know it already, don't you?"

"Keegan...he freaked...said he knew I'd mated with you."

His face hardened. "And that's when he broke your neck. Because of *me*." He whirled away from her.

"No!" She grabbed his arm. Swung him right back around. "He hurt me because he's an evil bastard. That's the same reason he hurt Harris. The same reason his pack came after us all so hard. You didn't do it. He did."

And Connor was nothing like Keegan.

Her shoulders sagged as the moonlight fell down on her. "What am I going to do? I-I don't...I just don't know what's coming. If the silver sensitivity returns again, that means the wolf is still inside me. *But I could never fully shift. Will I just get stuck again? Trapped in limbo?*" Trapped in that hell forever?

"Holly will help you." He sounded so confident of that.

She wanted to believe him. Chloe stared up at him. "Is it really true what they say about vampires?"

"People say plenty about vampires, and I'm not exactly a normal vamp."

No, he wasn't. "Can you control people?" Eric had wanted him to control her, but Connor had refused.

The idea of that much power...the idea that someone out there could *do* that...

He nodded. "I can."

Goosebumps rose on her arms.

"And we've got a big damn problem on our hands, because that guy out there—Keegan? I think he's like me, Chloe."

She stumbled back a step.

"Silver didn't hurt him. It didn't slow him down. So I think he's changed, too. As far I know...well, as far as I knew...Duncan and I were the only two cross-overs."

"A cross-over? Is—is that what you are?"

"That's what Eric has been calling us. A crossed mix of vampire and werewolf. A super beast."

Her body seemed to have iced. "How did Keegan change?"

"It's not easy, but maybe the senator helped him. We already know the guy was doing a lot of experiments, so maybe Keegan was one of the senator's projects. Maybe he amped up his power. Maybe—" Connor stopped. "Shit."

"Connor?"

"Maybe that was the plan all along. The senator wanted the paranormals to come out, to show the humans just how strong they were, but what's stronger than a werewolf? Stronger than a vampire?"

He was running back toward the building. "Connor!"

He looked back at her. "Cross-overs. A vampire can't be made into a werewolf, but a werewolf can become a vampire...all of the strengths, and none of the silver weakness. It's not supposed to happen. But Eric figured out it *could* happen, if the werewolf was an alpha. The alphas are strong enough to last through the change. They're strong enough—"

"To cross-over," Chloe finished.

"Maybe that's why your father wanted so many powerful vamps and werewolves sent to Purgatory. Not to keep the streets safer for humans, but so that he could see if they could cross-over. Fuck, he could have set up the prison just to make his own damned army!"

An unstoppable army.

He offered his hand to Chloe. "Come on, we need to find Eric, right now."

***

"Are you going to kill him if his wolf takes over?"

Eric had known that Duncan would ask that question, sooner or later. The guy had obviously opted for sooner.

They were in the hall, right outside of Harris's room. The agent was still strapped down and collared. He shouldn't be a threat to anyone then.

Shouldn't.

"Hopefully, I won't have to make that decision." Because he was going to bet on Harris. The man could prove himself to be a fighter.

Before Duncan could say anything else, Eric heard the rapid pound of approaching footsteps. He looked up and saw Connor and Chloe heading toward him.

The expression on Connor's face told him this wasn't going to be a friendly little chat.

"Did she die again already?" Eric asked, shaking his head. "Hell, man, I told you to keep her safe—"

Connor's low, lethal growl cut through his words. "You knew what they wanted from Purgatory, didn't you?"

Careful now, Eric said, "A war? Yes, I've told you for a while now that forces are working to stir up the paranormals, to—"

"You were against Purgatory. You told me before that you thought it was dangerous."

"Putting all the most powerful paranormals together in one place is a recipe for disaster." He kept the emotion out of his voice and he shrugged. "But I was out voted originally." His gaze slid to Chloe. "Other, more powerful voices held sway with the government. My job was to follow their orders."

"The senator's voice," Connor charged.

Eric nodded. "His was the loudest at the time. He told everyone that putting the paranormals in prison was far more humane than outright killing them. And he convinced the powers that be that we needed *one* prison for a test run."

"They're trying to cross-over, aren't they?" Connor demanded.

"I hope the fuck not," Duncan muttered.

Chloe just watched them argue. He saw her gaze dart between them all.

"Crossing-over isn't that easy. If it was, the ground would already be thick with other bastards like you two." Eric waved his hand toward them. "*I* have security in charge at the prison. The werewolves are separated from the vampires at all times. They don't have the chance to try and power up each other. Fuck, why would the vamps *want* to do that? If they bit the werewolves, if they actually found an alpha who could survive being near death *and* then getting a surge of vampire blood…well, they'd just be making a super beast that could kill them."

But Connor just glared at him, and Eric realized the guy wasn't buying the story. *Yes, join the freaking club. Not like I buy it either.* "I pushed for separate prisons, it didn't happen." *Because you're right...the senator did want to make cross-overs, but it's not that easy of a task. It's a one in a million shot.*

Connor had survived and so had his brother Duncan. There had been others that the government had experimented on...other alpha werewolves.

They hadn't transitioned. They'd died—horrible, painful deaths.

So while the others thought it was just about being an alpha, Eric knew the truth. More was at work...and that was why he had his scientists studying Connor and Duncan's DNA. They were brothers, and with both of them being cross-overs...*the key has to be within them.*

He hadn't told Holly about his research yet. Mostly because he didn't want her to freak out when she realized he was studying her lover, but soon, he'd have to pull her in. She was the best in the field of paranormal genetics, and he needed her help.

"You're worrying for no reason," he told Connor with another shrug. "You and Duncan are the only two who have managed—"

"Keegan is just like us."

Eric didn't let his surprise show. "That's not possible." *It had better not be possible.*

"It is...I saw him with my own eyes. Silver didn't burn him. He had fangs! He was just like us." Connor glared at him. "And if he can transform, others out there can, too. Purgatory is a powder keg, and if we don't do something soon, it will explode."

Didn't the guy think he was working on that shit? "I have guards there. They are making absolutely certain that the prisoners are contained at all times. The vampires are separate from the werewolves. And, again, they *can't* cross-over, even if they broke out into all-out brawls."

"Then explain Keegan to us."

"I can't, not yet." He thrust back his shoulders. "So that means getting that guy into custody is our number one priority. The sooner we have him on Holly's exam table, the sooner we can figure out just what the hell is going on."

His gaze slid to Chloe. She looked so fragile, and there was no missing the worry in her eyes. Hell, the woman had died that day, and while he'd played his part before when they'd been in the lab, sympathy did push through him as he gazed at her. Others might think he didn't have a heart, but it was there.

Just buried deep.

"You should get some rest," he said to Chloe. Because, unfortunately, in order to get Keegan, they'd be using her. "Dawn will come all too soon."

He inclined his head to Connor and Duncan. "Gentlemen, we'll plan to meet again at 0800." He turned from them.

Headed down the hallway.

He wasn't particularly surprised to hear footsteps following him. Connor's hand flew out and grabbed his arm right before Eric went into his office.

"Do you think I don't know?" Connor said, his voice low and rasping.

Tread carefully. Eric let his brows climb as he looked at Connor. "Know?"

"You were *bitten* at Eclipse. I saw it happen, man." And the guy sounded as if he cared. How touching. "What can we do? Does Holly know? Does—"

He stepped back, sliding away from Connor's hold. "You're mistaken. Sure, that wolf was coming at me with fangs bared, but he never bit me. I broke his jaw." He shrugged as he walked toward his desk. "End of story."

"Then why do I smell your blood?"

Damn enhanced senses.

"Because I was cut in the battle," he said smoothly, "but not bit. Save your worry for Chloe. I'm fine."

Connor marched into his office. "Why do I need to worry for Chloe? What the hell have you got planned?"

Ah, now anger was in the guy's voice.

"We have to bring in Keegan," he said. This should be obvious. "To get him, we have to use something he wants."

Right then, the only thing he seemed to want was Chloe.

"Sonofabitch," Connor muttered.

Chloe entered his office. She'd sidled up behind Connor. She looked between the two men, and Eric could practically feel her nervousness. "You should get some rest," he told Chloe. "There's a...lot coming." Talk about a serious understatement.

She headed toward his desk. Her hands flattened on the surface and she stared into his eyes. "Is there any chance that I can ever live a normal life again?"

He didn't look away from her. "I've always thought normal was way over-rated."

She swallowed.

Connor's hand curled over her shoulder. "Come on, Chloe."

Her fingers slid over Eric's desk. She didn't speak again, but Connor did. He stopped on the threshold and looked at Eric. "You don't want to see what happens if I'm pushed too far."

Actually, no, he didn't want to see that.

Connor shut the door. When Eric was sure that no one else was about to barge into his office, he took off the coat he'd grabbed from his SUV. The coat that had been covering him the entire time he'd been in Holly's lab. The coat had gotten soaked with blood, and he had to pry it away from his shoulder.

Without the jacket, the holes in his shirt were obvious. The werewolf's fangs had torn deep into him when the guy had made that bite.

Fuck.

It was a good thing he'd prepared for this situation…He wouldn't be transforming. At least, not any more than he'd changed in the past.

CHAPTER TEN

Chloe wasn't talking.

And Connor didn't know what the hell he should say to her.

They were back in the room she'd been given at the Para Base. Chloe was sitting on the bed, her shoulders hunched, staring down at her hands.

Eric was planning to use her. To dangle her as pretty bait to pull in that bastard Keegan.

I can't let that happen.

Because the last time that Chloe had gone out on one of Eric's missions, she'd died in front of Connor. There was no way he could let that happen again. It *wouldn't* happen.

"I know what he's planning." Chloe's head tilted back, and she stared up at him. "You don't need to stand there and try to figure out a way to tell me."

"Chloe…"

"It's obvious. If Keegan really is like you and Duncan, then Eric will do anything he deems necessary in order to bring the guy in. So he'll use me and try to get Keegan to come rushing into whatever trap he has planned." She stood up. "But Keegan doesn't want to do anything but kill me. I mean, that's obvious right? He broke my neck the last time he saw me. I don't think the fellow is exactly driven wild by love for me."

"I think he is driven wild," Connor said carefully. "By jealousy." And this was on him. Connor crossed the narrow room to stand by her side. "I marked you, and he knows it." His hand sank beneath the curtain of her hair. "If I'd kept my hands off you—" He broke off, because he didn't want to say the rest.

Her sad smile told him that she already knew. "Then *he* would have marked me? Right? You think he wants me? As a mate?"

Yes, he did.

"But I can't even shift, I—" Her eyes widened. "My scent. That's what you've all been talking about. What David Vincent was saying. My father changed my scent so that the male wolves would be drawn to me."

Like a moth to a fucking flame.

"But now the scent is different," Chloe said. "Because you marked me."

Grimly, Connor nodded.

She jerked back. "Oh, my God." Her hands wrapped around her stomach. "You—you didn't even want me, not really, did you? It's all about that stupid scent! Whatever, he did to me, it messed with your wolf's instincts. You didn't even want—"

"Let's get one thing real clear."

She gazed up at him.

"I want you more than I've ever wanted anyone in this world. I told you, your scent didn't work on me the same way because I'm part vamp. So me, wanting you…" He nodded. "That is just me wanting you. Me needing you more than I need anything else."

"Th-that's the way I feel about you. I wanted to be with you. Wanted to know what it was like to give in to a desire like that, just once."

"Once isn't all we'll have." Because he had no intention of letting her go.

And right there, in that little room, the memories surrounded him. He'd had her on that bed. Been driven out of his head by her touch and her silky body. He wanted her then. Always. Wanted to plunge into her again and again.

"Connor?"

His jaw was clenched and his cock shoved against the front of his jeans.

"You can compel me, can't you?"

"I haven't." He didn't want her to think that her desire for him hadn't been real. The feelings they shared—they were one hundred percent real.

"But…you can. Vampires can compel their victims if they take their blood."

Yes, that was how it worked. But he'd tried to be so careful. Always keeping his bloodlust in check. He knew that werewolf blood was supposed to be particularly dangerous, particularly addictive, to vampires.

"I've never compelled anyone," he said. "And I don't plan—"

"I want you to compel me."

Now she'd shocked him.

"I want you to compel me, and then I want you to teach me how to resist the compulsion."

"Baby, that can't be done."

She rubbed her arms. "It has to be done. Because if Keegan is like you, then—then he can compel me, too. I have to be able to break away if he tries. I don't want to wind up being some kind of sick puppet for him."

Now he had to touch her again. The pain in her voice pierced right through him. "I'm not going to let that happen."

"What if you can't stop him? What if no one can? I don't know how big his pack is. That's why Eric wanted him brought in, right? To break up that power network?"

One of the many reasons.

And I just want to kick his ass for what he's done to you.

"Compel me," Chloe said, her voice urgent. "Teach me how to resist."

His fangs were stretching in his mouth. "He can't compel you unless he drinks your blood. That *won't* happen." He wasn't going to let that bastard get close to Chloe again. Screw whatever plan Eric *thought* he'd use. Chloe wasn't going to be put at risk.

"I'm going to leave," Chloe said, raising her chin. "I'm going to walk out that door and out of this base. I'm going to keep going. You won't find me, but he might." And she pulled away from him. Headed for the door.

"Chloe!"

"Stop me," she said, without looking back.

He caught her arm and spun her around. "I don't have to compel you to stop you." He had easily over a hundred pounds on her. *Plus* werewolf and vamp power. "You're not going out there."

"I need to see what it feels like," Chloe told him. Her blue gaze was stark. "If I don't know, then how can I prepare for him? I want to be ready."

She jerked against his hold. Opened her mouth and *screamed.*

"Chloe, shit, stop!"

She screamed louder.

He clamped his hand over her mouth. "What are you trying to do?" Connor demanded. "Bring a ton of guards racing up here?"

Her gaze held his.

No, hell, he knew exactly what she was trying to do.

"You're not going to like it," he whispered. "Baby, I don't want to do this." His hand slid away from her mouth.

"I need to know what it feels like," Chloe argued, her delicate jaw set. "I have to know what I'm up against."

She wasn't backing down. And maybe…maybe she did need to see what it would be like if she was trapped under a compulsion. *I just don't want to do this! I never want to hurt her.* "Okay." He fucking hated this. Connor rolled back his shoulders. He sucked in a deep breath. And he looked into her eyes. "*Chloe…*"

He could feel the power rising within him, a darkness that he'd never felt before. One that tempted, one that whispered so seductively…one that wanted him to use the link he'd forged through blood.

One that wanted him to control Chloe.

She blinked and her gaze became a little unfocused. "C-Connor?" Fear flashed on her face.

"You're not going to fight me," he told her. He could damn well feel that surge of dark power within him, seeming to heat his veins. "You're going to walk to the bed and you're going to sit down on the mattress."

She stood there, and, for a moment, he could see the struggle in her expression. Then she took one step and stopped, shaking her head.

Well, well…

According to everything he'd learned, humans were supposed to be easy to control. Werewolves took more effort.

"Go to the bed, Chloe."

Her breath came faster. There was no emotion showing in her eyes now, those bright eyes of hers looked blank, but the struggle was plain to see on her face.

He *hated* this.

She took one step. Another. He kept focusing on her.

And she went to the bed. Sat down.

Waited. Just waited for him to tell her what to do next.

His claws were out. Would this really be what it was like if Keegan got control of her? He could just take her blood and make her do anything? The images that flashed through Connor's head had him snarling as he stalked toward Chloe.

But she didn't move.

Just waited.

"Offer your neck to me." The words came out unbidden. Because something was happening inside of Connor. The more he used that dark compulsion, the more he could feel his control fracturing.

This was Chloe. She was his. He'd marked her in the way of the wolf, a sign that all other werewolves would recognize — they'd know she was his.

But that bastard Keegan had tried to take Chloe away.

No one can take her away.

She offered her neck to him. He could hear the fast beat of her heart. Could all but taste the warmth of her blood.

He leaned over her. Pressed his lips to her neck. Her skin was so soft and silken and her blood — her blood was nectar. How had he gone so long without tasting her? And now, now that he knew how good she'd be…why not take more? She'd enjoy it. Prey enjoyed the bite. Prey would —

She's not prey. She's Chloe. She's —

Everything.

Connor spun away from her. "Lesson over, okay? Fucking over." His hands pressed to his eyes as he fought to get his control the hell back.

So hard, when all he really wanted was to plunge his fangs into her throat and drive his cock into her warm, wet sex.

Behind him, Connor heard her inhale sharply. Then the floor creaked as she headed toward him.

"No, Chloe." A refusal, not a compulsion. "Don't touch me now. I don't have much control."

"I would have done anything you wanted." Her voice was soft, scared. "Anything. I tried to fight when you first told me to walk to the bed, but then…then it was as if I were just a puppet, moving right along to anything, everything you wanted."

"I stopped," he said, his own voice hoarse because his control was truly razor thin. "I never want to hurt you."

"He does. He will. And I won't be able to stop him."

Connor whirled toward her. "*I'll* stop him."

"You can't be with me every second. He tried to kill me before, he'll do it again." She shook her head. "And if he's realized that he can kill me over and over and over…is that what's waiting for me?"

"No." He held his body perfectly still. She wasn't touching him, and he couldn't touch her. "I'll kill him before that happens. I won't let him torture you." He sucked in a deep breath, and dammit, he could taste her. "We'll contain him. Lock him up." *Or kill him.* "He won't be a threat to you again."

"I never realized just how dangerous vampires could be."

"Not all vampires compel their prey." He never wanted to compel again. Because…there had been too much power in that particular darkness. Too much temptation to become something he didn't want to be.

I've got too much of my father in me.

"The vamps who compel and kill…their victims never have a chance, do they?"

No, they didn't.

"If you shoot a vamp in the heart with a wooden bullet," Connor knew his voice was still too rough, "that can stop a vamp in his tracks. Freeze him, and make him look and act as if he's dead."

"But…does that work on you? Silver doesn't hurt you, so do you still have a vamp's weakness for wood in the heart?"

"Sunlight doesn't slow me down," Connor confessed.

"Does the wooden bullet stop you?"

Grimly, he shook his head.

Her breath rushed out. "Then it won't stop him, either. Not if he's really like you."

There was another way. A fool-proof one. "Cut off his head," Connor said. "That stops werewolves and vampires."

Chloe stared up at him. "I'm scared."

So the fuck was he.

"I'm scared of him. I'm scared of what I've become, and Connor, I'm scared of you."

Shock held him still. *I terrified her. When I was using the compulsion…shit, now she looks at me as if—*

"I'm scared because I want you, Connor. I know you're dangerous, and I don't care. I look at you and I want." She wet her lips. "What does that say about me? When you were compelling me to offer my neck, I did…I moved automatically, but deep inside…I wanted you to bite me. I wanted you to taste my blood." She paused. "And I still do."

"Be careful…what you say…"

"It's just like before. I don't know what will happen when the sun rises. But I know what can happen right here, right now between us." Staring at him, she started to strip.

The woman knew he got weak when she did that. "Chloe—"

"You're not compelling me. I'm seducing you."

"You—you should rest. You should—"

"I want to be with you. Because there is no way that it was really that good before, right? I'll have sex with you again, and I won't feel the same way." Her shirt hit the floor. "I won't feel like my soul is touching yours. I won't feel like I *fit* you."

She was clad in just her bra and panties. When her hand moved to the clasp of her bra, he stopped her, catching both of her hands in his.

"You're making a mistake." His body curled around hers. His cock shoved against his jeans and wanted *in* her. So deep. He wanted to hear her scream for him.

"I don't have a soul," he told her. *If only.* "I lost that long ago." It had been clawed out of him.

But Chloe shook her head. "Liar," she accused then she rose onto her toes. Her mouth pressed to the curve of his shoulder and she —

Bit him. Marked him, right there, in the way of werewolves.

It was a shock to his system. Because that part of his body was damn sensitive and for Chloe to mark him there, for her to lick and bite and —

"You're mine now," Chloe told him, "just as I'm yours." Then she licked his neck.

His control *shattered*. The marking was primitive, elemental, and so was his response. He yanked her up against him, spun around and pinned her to the wall.

Chloe would have known…the one thing designed to rip through his control…the one thing that would call up his beast with a ferocious hunger…

To be marked.

Claimed.

He lifted her up higher and yanked away her panties. He could feel the spot she'd marked on his shoulder, it was warm, the heat spiraling through him.

"I want you to bite me," Chloe said, her voice a husky temptation. "It feels so good..."

Yes.

Her head tilted back. He wasn't compelling her. She was offering herself to him, and he couldn't resist her. His fingers pushed into her sex even as his fangs sank into her throat. Her taste was heaven on his tongue, and she was growing hotter and wetter against his fingers. Her hips arched toward him as she cried out his name.

A wave of power and euphoria swept through him. He thrust his fingers into her, but that wasn't enough. Not nearly.

He withdrew, pulled out his cock, and positioned her. He should go slower, take more care, but he couldn't.

The blood was burning in his veins. His thoughts had splintered and all he knew was her.

Take.

Mate.

Mine.

He sank into her and felt her come around him. Her sex squeezed him tight, nearly making him go insane. Her contractions slid around the length of his aroused flesh, driving his hunger higher, wilder...

And still he drank from her.

Chloe.

He locked his hands around her waist and lifted her against him. He held her there, moving her against his rocking hips. Then he licked her neck, kissing the wound he'd made.

She was still climaxing. Whispering his name and shuddering against him.

He let go then. Connor emptied himself in Chloe. He fucking got lost in her as his orgasm pounded through him.

When it ended, he carried her back to the bed. He tucked her in. Pressed a kiss to her lips.

And Connor knew he was well and truly fucked.

Nothing can happen to her…because I can't let her go.

Chloe was his, and he was hers. If Keegan tried to get her again, the bastard wouldn't live to see another sunset.

***

"Let me go…"

Connor opened his eyes. He'd fallen asleep in the chair next to Chloe's bed. He could have left her, but…he'd wanted to stay. Just in case she needed him.

"Chloe?"

She was twisting on the bed. *"I…like it here…"* Her head moved from the left to the right, twice, in a frantic shake. "Let me go…let me stay…it doesn't hurt here."

A chill skated up his spine. There was something about the way Chloe was talking…

"*So beautiful…*" Chloe whispered. "I want to stay. Let me go so I can stay!"

He reached out to her. Caught her hand in his. "Chloe, wake up."

She didn't. "Want to…stay…but…Connor?"

"Chloe, wake up." The chill was growing worse. He almost felt as if Chloe was slipping away from him, right then. "*Wake up!*"

She gave a little gasp and her eyes flew open. Her hand grabbed onto his. "Connor?"

He eased onto the side of the bed, needing to be closer to her. "You were having another nightmare."

She stared up at him. "A…a nightmare?" She tucked her hair behind her ear. "Right, a nightmare."

The unease he felt got worse. "Tell me about it?"

"I-I don't remember it." She pulled her hand from his. Grabbed the covers.

Connor didn't move. First, Chloe had dreamed of fire. Now, she dreamed of something else…something beautiful. "Where were you?" Connor asked, unable to hold the question back.

At first, he didn't think Chloe would answer him. He didn't want her to lie to him. Not again.

Connor never wanted any more lies between them. He wanted Chloe to be able to tell him anything.

"I don't know," Chloe finally said. "But it didn't hurt there. And I wasn't afraid."

He was afraid.

"No fire, no screams. It was peaceful."

"And you wanted to stay."

Her head turned on the pillow. She stared at him. "I thought I did." She bit her lip. "But then I remembered you. I wanted you more than I wanted to stay."

His chest burned.

"Will you...will you hold me for a little while?"

He climbed into that narrow bed with her. Positioned their bodies so that she was on top of him. The chill finally left Connor when her arms wrapped around him.

"Connor, what's the one thing you want most in life?"

He didn't know. His arms tightened around her.

Maybe I've found what I want.

"I don't want you to think I'm your jailer," he said, his voice rumbling.

"I don't think that, not anymore."

Silence.

He had to ask, "What do you want most?"

"To be free. To not be afraid of anyone or anything."

Then I'll find a way to make that happen for you.

He pressed a kiss to her temple and as the sun began to rise, he held her.

***

The Para Base had been quiet all night. But at dawn, an armored van left the facility. Keegan was watching closely, and the sight of that van immediately caught his attention.

"Well, well," he murmured. "Just who do we have running…?"

He left a team watching the base, men who were all staying back a safe distance, and he followed that van with a core group of his pack. When the van was far enough away from the base…he attacked.

He leapt onto the hood and drove his hand right through the front windshield. He grabbed the driver and yanked him out through the broken glass. He tossed that bleeding bastard across the street. The passenger was firing, but the idiot was shooting silver.

Doesn't work on me.

He drove his fist at that guy, too, shattering more glass. Soon the second man stopped firing.

Other members of his pack had closed in. They pried open the back door of that vehicle.

More guards were waiting inside, and their silver did work on two of the werewolves who were in front of Keegan. When they fell, he just walked over their bodies.

He knocked out the guards. Easy enough.

Then he saw the prisoner who was inside that vehicle. A man who was chained up. Smiling at him.

David Vincent. His former pack leader.

David said, "Hurry, hurry! Get me out of here!"

His claws tapped against the side of the door. Did the fool really think he could still give orders? "You're not alpha anymore. You're not even a werewolf." He was a waste of space.

But then, Keegan hadn't attacked the van in order to save any prisoners. He'd attacked because he had a plan. *I take the van, then I can use it to just drive right into the Para Base.* The fools there would just think their own men were returning in the vehicle.

He'd get in the base, easy as pie.

He'd have to repair the windshield, of course, but with his resources, that wouldn't be hard. Then...then he'd just slip right inside the base.

Too simple. So perfect.

He stalked toward David.

And the guy finally got a damn clue. Because David's eyes widened in horror and he pressed back against the side of that armored van. "No, no, you don't understand! You don't—"

The *rat-a-tat* of gunfire cut through the night. Keegan spun around just as bullets blasted into him. Not silver bullets, but tranq darts.

"Learned that one from you," a mocking voice called out. "And by the way, dumbass, you're kind of easy to predict."

A tall male with green eyes appeared at the back of the armored van.

Keegan's knees gave out beneath him, and he sank onto the floor of the van. "Lock him in," the man ordered.

David Vincent started laughing. That mocking sound grated in Keegan's ears.

Armed men jumped in the back of the vehicle. They locked restraints around his wrists and ankles.

"The rest are werewolves," Keegan heard the man—the leader—shout. He recognized the bastard as Eric Pate. "Put them in silver collars and we'll transport them all back to base."

Then Eric jumped into the armored van. He closed in on Keegan, and the guy kicked him in the side.

"Hey," Eric snapped. "Don't go out on me, not yet."

It was hard to keep his eyes open.

"Really, you'd think you were the only one who knew how to cloak a scent. Hell, I'm the one who invented that shit. Someone just stole my product and gave it to you." Eric kicked him again.

Keegan howled in pain.

"That's for biting my agent. I don't take kindly to people attacking my team." Eric bent down toward him. His voice dropped to a low, lethal whisper. "And I really get pissed off when some jerk kills a woman on my watch." Eric locked his fingers around Keegan's neck. "So I'm thinking...maybe it'll be *your* time to die soon."

Keegan tried to reply, but his tongue had gone thick in his mouth. He couldn't speak, couldn't move. All he could do was listen to the grating sound of David Vincent's laughter.

That prick is the first to die when I'm free.

Doors slammed shut a few minutes later. The vehicle lurched forward.

The drugs that had been pumped into him made Keegan a prisoner in his own body. He wanted to move, but he couldn't. He wanted to fight, but his claws weren't even coming out.

"So much for being an alpha, huh, asshole?" David Vincent taunted. "You didn't even see the trap coming for you. And now, it's too late."

Is it?

He couldn't move, but Keegan could plan.

CHAPTER ELEVEN

A knock sounded at the door. He woke instantly, his body fully alert.

"Connor?" Chloe murmured. "What's happening?"

"*Connor!*" Eric's yell. "I need you, now."

Hell. He pressed a kiss to Chloe's lips. "Stay here, baby. I'll be right back." He grabbed his jeans, yanked them on, then pulled on a t-shirt. When he opened the door, he made sure not to open it wide enough for Eric to see inside. Connor sure didn't want the guy getting an eyeful of a naked Chloe.

"About time," Eric muttered. "Man, you are slow as shit."

Connor glared at him. "And you are *always* pounding on our damn door. You know what you need, Eric? A date. A woman. You need to have issues of your own."

Eric turned on his heel. "I need you downstairs."

Connor hesitated.

"Chloe is fine." Now Eric sounded annoyed. "And as your boss, I'm giving you an order...*come downstairs.*"

Connor followed, but he wasn't happy about it.

Only Eric didn't stop at the first level of the base. He went all the way down to containment.

"We got some new prisoners this morning. I thought you might want to see them..." Eric typed in his passcode and the doors to the containment area slid open. "Oh, and by the way, you can thank me with a case of beer later."

Connor's shoulders stiffened as he saw the werewolves. At least a dozen of them. All in silver cages. All wearing silver collars.

"We rounded up all the ones who followed my little bit of bait and the ones who'd stayed behind to keep surveillance running on this place." Eric sauntered toward the cages. "Like I didn't realize they were out there, watching. That shit was just insulting. What kind of security do they think I have? With the way things went the last few months, I stepped up *everything.*"

Some of those werewolves smelled familiar. *They were at Eclipse.* He whirled back to Eric. "They're Keegan's pack."

Eric nodded.

"You knew they were watching the base? With Chloe here?" He shot forward. "What the hell—"

"I didn't transfer Chloe immediately because I wanted them to watch the place. I needed them to stay close so I could keep up my surveillance on them." Eric said this as if it should have been obvious. "And my trap worked."

He was going to hurt Eric. In so many ways.

"Sheath your claws and I'll show you just how well it ended."

He could barely growl out a response. But Eric had just turned on his heel and headed down a narrow hallway.

Toward maximum security containment.

Silver doors barred the way. Artificial sunlight pumped into the area.

"Of course, these containment measures aren't stopping him, so we're having to keep the prisoner sedated, for the time being. Until other…means…can be discovered to neutralize the threat he poses."

They eased around a corner, but Connor had already caught the bastard's scent. Rage fueled his blood, and it took every ounce of power that Connor had to not race across the room and kill the guy in that cell.

Keegan was there. His arms were shackled. His legs secured. His head sagged forward.

For an instant, the world went red for Connor. He stared at Keegan and his claws stretched from his fingertips. He had never wanted to kill anyone more, not even his bastard of a torturing father.

"Keep that control," Eric warned him. "Hell, your reaction right now is the reason I didn't take you out on the mission with us. I worried that if you went with that team—"

"You wouldn't bring that bastard in alive."

He wanted to rip through those bars and attack Keegan.

At that moment, Keegan's head tilted back. He stared at Connor out of bleary eyes, and the guy grinned.

Oh, the hell, no.

Eric slapped his hand on Connor's chest. "*Don't.* I need him alive, got it? I have to see how many werewolves are involved in the mess the senator left behind. I have to find out how the hell Keegan managed to become a cross-over."

"He needs to be in the ground." Connor was definite on this. "After what he did to Chloe, there's no question of what we should do to him."

Eric sighed. "Things aren't always black and white. You of all people know that."

Connor knocked his hand away.

"He's in custody," Eric said. "He can't hurt Chloe again. He won't hurt anyone. It's over for him."

"So what? He gets a fast trip to Purgatory? Don't you get it, Eric? That's probably what he wants!"

"I'm going to interrogate him soon. I'll find out every secret the guy has."

Eric thought he was the one in control.

But Keegan was still grinning.

And Connor wanted to rip his head off.

"He's contained," Eric told him. "That's a good thing. A win. Chloe doesn't need to be afraid any longer."

But then Keegan said… "Yes, she does." His voice was low, rasping. "Because I'll be…leaving this place…soon…and my Chloe will come with me."

Connor raced forward. He wanted to sink his claws deep into Keegan's chest, but when he touched the cage, an electric surge shot through him.

He snarled at the flash of pain.

"That's some new, enhanced security we have." Eric's voice was flat. "You aren't killing him. Not when I've gone to such trouble to bring the guy in alive."

He wanted that bastard *dead*.

"You can let Chloe know that the threat to her has been eliminated."

The threat hadn't been eliminated, not yet. It had just been brought right to her. Up-close and personal.

Connor whirled on his heel and marched away from Keegan. He had to leave, if he didn't—he would be killing that werewolf.

"She isn't clear yet, agent," Eric said. "Chloe can't leave the facility."

Connor stopped.

"Just didn't want you getting any ideas."

Connor glanced back at Eric.

"Chloe Quick is still a person of extreme interest for the Para Unit. She might not be in a containment cell, but that doesn't mean she can walk free."

Connor shook his head. "You really are a bastard, you know that, Eric?"

"Never pretended to be anything else," Eric murmured. "Brief Chloe and then...then I'll be transferring Keegan to Holly's lab for tests. You might want to stop by for that part."

Why? Because if Keegan broke free, only Connor and Duncan had a chance of matching the guy in a power fight? "You realize you could be making a serious mistake."

Eric didn't speak.

Right. Shaking his head, Connor walked the fuck away.

***

"He's...here?" Chloe asked. Her knees were shaking. She really hoped Connor hadn't noticed that tremble because she was trying to appear brave and in control.

But she was seriously shaking apart.

"Eric has him in a special containment area. From the look of things, Eric brought in most of the guy's pack."

She should be relieved. Keegan wasn't out there, hunting her any longer. *No, now he's in the building with me.*

"I want to leave," Chloe blurted.

Connor stared back at her.

He's not my jailer. He's my lover.

"Let's both leave," Chloe said and she knew she sounded a bit desperate. That was fair, she felt desperate. "You and me. Let's just leave this place and go start over somewhere new."

He wasn't speaking.

"You said I was your last assignment. Well, can't we consider the assignment done? Finished? Eric brought in the bad guy, and the streets are safe." She ran a hand through her hair. "Now we can go out and live a normal life, just like everyone else." The farther she was from Keegan, the better she would feel. "We can leave today. We can go out and vanish and just—"

"No," Connor said quietly.

Her heart was racing too fast. "You don't want to leave with me?"

"Leaving now isn't an option. Not for either of us."

She shook her head. "I haven't done anything wrong." Other than kill her father. *But he killed me...he hurt me for so long.* Like that eased her guilt. "I haven't done anything to the Para Unit."

Connor's face looked as if it had been carved from stone.

"I want to be with you, Connor." She wasn't going to lie or pretend. She was going to tell him exactly how she felt. "When I'm with you, no matter what, I feel safer." But Chloe shook her head because it was about so much more than safety. "I feel good. As close to happy as I've ever been." Because Connor made her feel normal. He treated her like a woman and not some broken thing.

"I want to be with you." His voice was gravel-rough. "But we can't leave, not yet."

We. "I want to leave Connor. I don't want to stay here with him." This was the perfect time for her to vanish, didn't Connor see that? Keegan couldn't follow her now. She would be free.

"I know, but you can't leave."

Goosebumps rose on her arms. "Connor?"

"You haven't been given the all-clear yet. To the Para Unit, you're still a...a person of extreme interest."

"I'm a prisoner?"

He strode toward her. Took her hands in his. "You're with me, Chloe."

But she pulled away from him. "I don't want to be here anymore. I want to go. I want to live my life. Be free." Only she was starting to wonder, would that be possible?

Connor's gaze was tormented.

"Will I ever be free?" she asked him. "Really free?" Or would Eric always be keeping tabs on her?

"Baby…"

In that instant, Chloe made a decision. She straightened her shoulders and pulled away from him. "You want me, don't you, Connor?"

"You know I do."

Want. Lust. Need. That wasn't enough for her.

"I want you, too." She would hold nothing back. "But the thing is…I think I could love you."

His expression didn't change.

She held her breath and asked, "Do you think you could love me?"

"Chloe…"

"Someone told me…" Her voice was too brittle but she forced herself to continue. "That maybe we all deserve the chance to love and be loved. I want my chance, Connor. I want it with you."

His expression became even harder. "You want us to run away together."

"I want us to try having a life! I want the white, picket fence and barbecue nights! I want laughter and little league!" All of her dreams tumbled out right then. Dreams she'd had as a sixteen year old girl, before her life had turned into a living hell. Dreams that she'd thought were dead and buried.

But, apparently, nothing about her could stay dead. Not even those pesky dreams.

"I can't give you that."

Her heart hurt.

"I can't ever give you any of that." He shook his head. "Because you know what, Chloe? I am a monster. I have been from the time I was a child."

"No—"

"And that is who I will always be. I can't give you what you want."

She hurried forward and grabbed his arms. "I want you to love me."

"Baby, I don't know how to love."

His words sank right through her.

"I know how to kill and how to hurt. There's not much more to me than that."

"You're wrong." But he was hurting her right then. Crushing her. Turning her faint dreams to dust. "Give us a chance. Please, Connor, I'm begging you." Because she knew this was it. Her chance. Their chance. "Let's leave here. Let's go together, now, and leave everyone else behind. Let's—"

"I'm not leaving."

His words were so cold and so...final.

Her hands fell away from him.

"You're safe here, Chloe. You have my word on that."

And Connor never lied. She did. She lied often.

But I didn't lie about the way I feel. She was falling for him. Apparently, he was just fucking her.

"Now I need to go check in with Holly and Shane. Stay settled up here, and I'll be back to check on you soon."

Then, without another word, he just left her. The door closed softly behind him.

Chloe stared at the door. How could he not see it? There weren't bars on the room, but she was in a cell. She'd been captive most of her life.

I'm going to be free.

She wasn't going to be the weak one anymore. The one who was pushed around and hurt. She wasn't going to wait for someone else to decide her fate. Those days were over — and all she'd gotten for her trouble was blood, pain, and life as a semi-werewolf.

She rolled back her shoulders. She was getting out of this place. And she'd be getting out that day.

Good-bye, Connor. Because she would miss him. Always.

But she wouldn't give up her life for him.

***

Connor shoved open the door to Holly's lab. He wasn't particularly surprised to see the crowd that had gathered inside. "Looks like the gang is all here," he muttered.

Holly stood a few feet away, garbed in green scrubs. Duncan was at her side, like the guy always was. But if Eric was really going to have Holly run tests on Keegan, Connor had been sure that he'd find his brother in the room.

Shane was there, too. The vamp's expression was carefully schooled, but his body was tight. He might not look worried, but Connor knew the fellow was.

Olivia paced a few feet away. Nervous energy rolled off her body.

"Did you all know that Eric was bringing the bastard in?" Connor demanded.

"No," Duncan said immediately. "I didn't."

Shane shook his head. "I'm not in the loop anymore."

Holly sighed. "Eric thinks he doesn't have to answer to anyone."

"He's wrong," Connor said flatly.

Holly glanced back toward the door. "He's going to be bringing Keegan in any moment. I don't...I don't think you want to be here for this part."

"Hell, yes, I do." But that was a lie. He actually wanted to be on a motorcycle, with Chloe holding tight to him, as they rode hell-fast out of there.

So why am I here?

Chloe's image flashed in his mind. Her eyes had been so blue, her expression so stark. *Do you think you could love me?*

He didn't know anything about love. He knew about hate. About rage. About possession and obsession.

Love?

Hell, did it even exist?

"How's Harris?" Connor asked as he tried to shove the image of Chloe from his mind.

Duncan approached him. "He made it through the night. That's something."

Yeah, it was.

"But you know Eric. He wanted the guy put in a cell, just until the full moon passed. With it coming tonight, he didn't want to take any chances."

Connor had already felt the pull of the moon.

"Connor, if you're going to attack Keegan, you know you can't stay in here."

Connor cracked his knuckles. "I'll play nicely…"

"Are you sure you know how?" This came from Shane.

Connor gave him a hard glare. "I'll play nicely...as long as he stays under Eric's control. If the bastard makes an attempt to attack, he's done." Because Connor couldn't allow Keegan to threaten Chloe again.

Chloe.

The woman was haunting him right then. She'd been so hopeful, but he truly wasn't the barbecue and picket fence type. His instincts were too dark. Too dangerous.

Chloe hadn't seen the real Connor, not yet. She thought he was one of the good-guy agents. She just didn't get it.

And maybe I don't want her to get it. Maybe I want her to keep looking at me with that light in her eyes.

Because when she really saw him for the beast that he was, Chloe wouldn't think that she could fall in love with him. Chloe would run as fast and as hard as she could—as she tried to get away from him.

***

Chloe's fingers slipped beneath the mattress. When Connor had stormed into Eric's office late last night, she'd tagged along. And while Connor had questioned Eric, she'd helped herself to one of Eric's precious keycards.

So maybe she had some sticky fingers. Maybe she'd had to escape the guards her father had put on her over the years.

She'd stared right into Eric's eyes as she'd palmed the keycard off his desk. For someone who was supposed to be so savvy, Eric had sure not even noticed her little theft routine.

Her hand curled around the keycard. She'd been watching closely each time she was led through the facility. So she should be able to get back down to the lower level, using that keycard at all the right intervals, no problem. Then she'd find her way out and vanish.

She wouldn't see Connor again. She wouldn't see Olivia.

She'd be on her own.

Would she change into a wolf again? Chloe didn't know, but she *did* know that she couldn't stay in that base. She wanted a life, and she'd take it.

She opened her door. No guard stood on the other side. Connor must have really thought that she was fine with being a prisoner at that place. Pain gnawed through her.

Why couldn't he have come with me? But more, it seemed as if the real question was…*Why couldn't he have chosen me?* Because she felt as if it had been a choice for him.

Her…or the Para Unit.

She slid into the hallway. She could hear voices coming from the stairwell. Squaring her shoulders, Chloe took a deep breath. This was it.

She kept a tight grip on that keycard and headed down the stairs.

***

"Keep him sedated," Eric ordered the guards as they strapped Keegan to a gurney. "I don't want this jerk getting any chance to slip away from us."

The guards dosed Keegan again. Good. Eric nodded. Then he turned on his heel. He had to make sure that Holly was ready for her latest patient. As he swept out of the general containment area, his gaze slid to the right. Harris Grey was there, watching him. The silver collar seemed to glow around Harris's neck.

Eric paused. "The collar is just for your protection." And for the protection of every staff member in that base. "After the full moon passes, we'll know that you control your beast."

Harris was sitting in the middle of the cell. "And if the beast controls me...what then? You going to put me down? Ship me off to Purgatory?"

"I'll deal with you." That was all he'd say because the last thing Eric wanted to do was hurt a loyal agent.

He marched out of the area. Hell, he sure hoped Holly was ready for Keegan. Because they had to figure out how the guy had become a cross-over.

No one else can be allowed to change.

Cross-overs were far too dangerous.

***

The drugs were filling his veins. Cold, like ice that chilled him from the inside. The guards had strapped him down on the gurney, securing him so tightly. Too tightly, but they hadn't cared.

Now they were wheeling him out of the cell. His head sagged to the side, and he knew that he looked as if he were barely conscious.

Appearances could be so very deceiving.

They took him past his men. Werewolves locked down in their collars. He muttered as he past them, his voice no more than a whisper.

It was a good thing werewolves had such wonderful hearing.

The guards took him past another cell. One that was far away from the others. Ah…and there was someone in that cell, too. The agent he'd slashed…and bit.

When he saw Keegan, Harris jumped to his feet and ran forward with a yell.

"Easy, man, easy," one of Keegan's guards said.

"You bastard!" Harris yelled. "You damn, sick—"

"Get Chloe," Keegan murmured. He knew his words would be too soft for the human guards to hear. Luckily, Harris wasn't human any longer. "Kill her."

But when Chloe died...

Will you come back again? He was sure that she would, and he'd be ready.

Her death would be all the distraction he needed.

Harris's face went slack with shock. His furious gaze iced over, all emotion vanishing in an instant.

If he could have, Keegan would have smiled. It was really true what folks said about vamps and compulsion.

A little blood could go such a long way.

***

Eric burst into the lab.

Connor tensed when he saw the guy—and, yeah, Eric tensed when he saw Connor, too.

Eric pointed at Holly. "Are you ready for this?"

"Ready as I'll ever be," she muttered back.

Eric's gaze swept the room. "Everyone, stay at attention. He's drugged, but we don't want to take any chances with him, got it?"

Oh, Connor definitely had it.

The doors opened again and guards wheeled in Keegan.

Connor took an instinctive step forward.

"Don't." It wasn't Eric holding him back this time, it was Olivia. She'd snuck up on him. Not many people — including strong paranormals — could do that. "Just let Holly take some samples." Her worried stare was on Keegan. "I don't like this. The whole set-up gives me a bad feeling."

You and me both. That was why he was there. Why he'd left Chloe even though it had felt like he was walking on nails with every step he took away from her.

Holly approached Keegan with a syringe in her hand.

And, even though he was sedated, Keegan laughed. "Don't you just…want to drink from me…? Would you like that…more? I know about you, pretty vamp."

How the hell did he know Holly was a vampire?

"Know about…all… of you," Keegan said, his voice slightly slurred.

Duncan stepped to Holly's side.

Keegan's bleary stare landed on him. "Don't look…like him…" Keegan said. "Your brother…does…"

That bad feeling of Connor's got worse.

Because Connor knew exactly who he looked like. Unfortunately. He was the spitting image of his father.

I became a cross-over. Duncan is a cross-over.

But their father hadn't been able to harness that power. He'd tried, by his own admission, but the guy had died only as a werewolf. Nothing more. Nothing less.

Right?

Holly sank a needle into Keegan's arm.

The bastard smiled weakly at her. "I'm going…to kill you…soon…" Keegan promised.

"The hell you are," Duncan swore.

CHAPTER TWELVE

She'd made it to the main floor. Her heart was about to break out of her chest. Chloe grabbed for a lab coat that had been left out on a desk and she slid it on, hoping the coat would make her blend in a bit better. Then she scooped up a clipboard and pretty much buried her nose in the thing. The less attention she attracted, the better.

Chloe came to the first barred door on the main floor. She figured this door had to lead to one of two places...sweet, wonderful freedom...or down to containment.

This *wasn't* the way Eric had taken her when he'd so annoyingly locked her up, so she was betting this path led to freedom.

She lifted the keycard up and swiped it. The light on the control pad flashed green.

Yes.

The bars slid back and the door opened. Chloe hurriedly stepped through that doorway. An armed guard was up ahead, but when he saw her, he just gave a curt nod.

There was one more barred door up ahead, and Chloe could swear that she smelled the scent of fresh air.

I'm going to be free.

Finally.

She just...why hadn't Connor come with her?

Chloe shoved that thought into the recesses of her mind, straightened her shoulders, and walked forward.

She was less than three feet away from that second barred door when she heard the screams. The guard jerked to attention and his gun came down, pointing toward her.

"No, wait, I—" Chloe began.

But he ran right past her. He headed back into the base because the screams were coming from inside. Long, loud, terrible screams. Screams filled with pain and fear.

Chloe swiped the keycard over the next pad.

The bars on that door slid back. Fresh air slid over her face.

And the screams continued.

Her eyes squeezed shut. "Dammit."

***

"What in the hell is that?" Shane demanded.

The screams were loud, piercing.

Eric whirled for the door. "We shouldn't be hearing screams. The prisoners are all in containment. We shouldn't—"

"Not the prisoners…" Keegan muttered. "Try…again…"

Connor pointed at Duncan. "Stay here. Make sure he doesn't get loose."

Duncan nodded. Connor already knew his brother would kill in an instant, if it meant keeping Holly safe.

Connor rushed for the door, with Olivia and Shane right at his side. Eric was a few steps ahead of them. Eric opened the door and when they raced into the hallway, Connor saw a dark-haired agent running toward him.

Blood streamed down the man's neck.

"H-he said he needed help…" More screams echoed from the hallway. "It was…H-Harris…he needed…help…I…opened his…collar…"

"Fuck." Eric yanked out a radio. "Lock down the facility. No one gets in or out, understand? And be on alert for Agent Harris Grey. He is to be considered a hostile right now. Arm all guns with silver and fire on contact."

Eric took out his own gun. Connor didn't have a gun, but his claws were at the ready. Olivia and Shane both had their fangs bared. They all advanced fast through the facility. They found more wounded agents. Some were on the ground, some were slumped against the walls.

Olivia rushed to help them.

Shane and Eric hurried into the containment area. When they opened the door, Connor could hear the sound of the werewolves howling in there.

He hurried inside after them. The werewolves were clawing at their glowing collars and slamming into the silver cell bars again and again. Their flesh was burning, and they were howling with the pain. But they weren't stopping.

"What in the hell is wrong with them?" Eric yelled as he pulled out a remote — a small box that Connor knew would control the silver collars. "Let's amp up the power there."

The wolves howled louder as more silver was pumped into their blood. Connor had once worn one of those collars. He knew exactly how painful the collar could be. The collars were filled with small needles, and those needles injected silver directly into the werewolves' blood.

The silver *should* have controlled them.

It wasn't.

"They're out of control," Shane said. "Look at them! They're maddened, they're —"

More flesh was burning and the wolves were howling in pain, but they still weren't stopping their attacks on the cells. They were fighting frantically for a freedom they couldn't win.

Understanding settled heavily over Connor. "They're compelled," Connor said as he backed away. "Sonofabitch! He was two steps ahead of you, Eric! He bit all of his wolves, in case you captured them! This way, they can never turn on him." He whirled for the door. "And he must be compelling Harris! That's why the guy is attacking the other agents!"

But...where was Harris?

"Chloe," Connor whispered. Fear tore into him and he ran, moving faster than he'd ever moved in his entire life. He raced through the base, whipped up the stairs and threw open the door to her room.

Only...Chloe wasn't in that room.

***

She needed a weapon, and she needed it right then.

Chloe had slipped back inside the base just in time to see Harris Gray attack the guard. The man had rushed at Harris with his gun, but the guard hadn't fired.

"Harris...is that you?"

Instead of answering, Harris had clawed the gun right out of the guard's hands.

Chloe was now ducked behind a pile of boxes and Harris...

"This is your fault," he yelled, his voice shaking. "I wouldn't be like this...if you'd just followed orders. It goes back to that first night, when you slipped away. You led them to me. They kidnapped me, they tortured me...because of you!"

She wasn't going to call out to him. If she did, that would be a dead giveaway to her location. But...*if he's turning into a werewolf, then aren't all of his senses enhanced? Maybe he can hear my heart beat. Smell my fear.*

She seriously needed a weapon. Serious-freaking-ly. She crawled forward. That looked like a silver knife up ahead. Had it fallen from the guard's belt when Harris attacked him? If she could just get to it...

Hard fingers curled around her ankle.

"I don't want to kill you," Harris told her, voice gravelly, "but I don't have a choice."

***

"He's going to die...out there," Keegan whispered. "You were...supposed to protect him...before...but you didn't."

The agent he knew to be Duncan McGuire glared at Keegan.

"I know..." Talking was hard, but Keegan pushed through the pain. The vampiress kept shoving her needles into him. Later, he'd be sure to shove his fangs into her. Again and again, until she had no blood left. "I know…you didn't keep him…in that closet with you…let your father…take him…he *hates* you for…that…"

"Duncan, how does he know about that?" The vampiress asked, worry making her voice sharp.

I know everything.

"He was…a sick freak…right?" Keegan had to push those words out. The drugs were still doing a number on him. "You…stayed quiet because…you were older…"

Duncan's hand locked around Keegan's jaw, and the guy made Keegan look at him. "Who told you this?"

"You…didn't make a sound…Connor screamed. He was…young…"

"Who told you?"

"Bet…Connor will scream again…" Soon, as soon as Connor found Chloe's broken body.

Then everyone would run to find Connor and Chloe. When that happened, Keegan would have the chance to get free. He just needed a little help. A little blood.

And to get the hell out of the restraints that bound him.

"Who. Told. You?"

The vampiress had already finished with her blood work. She'd know the truth soon, but why wait for her analysis? They could learn this part right now.

"Our…father told me…" How else did they think he'd become like them? It was all in the blood…though not their father's blood.

Their mother's.

Did Duncan and Connor even realize that she'd been a natural-born wolf? Not turned, but born?

"He killed…her…but it was her…her blood…that helped you…change." *Helped us change.*

"You're a damn liar," Duncan said. "My mother was human!" Rage and shock battled on the guy's face.

He shook his head. "Her…family…raised me…" She'd intended to send all of her boys to her family, but their mother hadn't been given that chance.

He'd grown up, always knowing exactly what he was. Always seeing it in the eyes of that bloody Marrok pack.

A bastard's twisted son. The son of the man who'd killed their precious girl.

Instead of being sheltered, the family had hated him.

And he'd hated them…right up to the moment when he'd killed them all.

Keegan had another small tidbit to share. "He's…killing Chloe."

"Connor would never —" The vampiress began.

He couldn't shake his head. Not with Duncan holding him so tightly and with the drugs pumping through his blood. "H-Harris," he rasped. "Let's see…if she can…come back… again…"

Because no one could get away with cheating death. Not that bitch. Not his brothers.

Duncan swore and reached for a radio that had been strapped to his hip.

***

Chloe screamed and kicked out at Harris, catching him in the face. She heard the crunch of bones, and she hated that sound but…*he's trying to kill me!* Her fingers had closed around the knife and she brought it up, putting that silver blade between her and Harris. "Stay back!" Chloe yelled at him.

Harris clamped his hands over his ears. "I hear him…again and again…can't stop him… *'Get Chloe. Kill her. Get Chloe. Kill her. Get Chloe'* — "

"Kill me. Yes, right, I get the idea." What she got was that the guy was being compelled. That *had* to be it, right? "I really don't want to hurt you anymore. You seemed like a decent guy before you changed, and I know it can suck when wolves bite you and your life goes to hell and — "

"*You know nothing!*" Harris roared.

"Really? Try telling that to a sixteen year old girl who gets attacked by a pack of wolves. I was bitten seven times. I don't think they wanted me to live, they sure didn't want me to transform." But she'd survived. *And I'm going to survive now.* Chloe knew Harris was going to follow the compulsion he was under. She would have done anything for Connor when he'd been compelling her.

So Chloe figured there were two ways out of this mess.

Option one: Kill Harris.

Not so good for Harris.

Option two: Knock him out. Because if the guy was unconscious, then he couldn't follow any compulsions.

Now, to just find a way to knock out the guy.

"I don't want to stab you," she told him.

"'*Get Chloe. Kill*'—"

She sliced him across the stomach. He yelled and stumbled back and Chloe leapt to her feet. Her gaze flew to the left, then the right. She grabbed a lamp from the guard's desk and held it like a baseball bat. She'd hit Harris and knock the guy out. She swung out—

He just yanked the lamp from her fingers.

"Silver *hurts*."

"Newsflash," she told him as she backed up. "It's going to hurt a whole lot worse once the full moon rises and your change is complete. You're still in the honeymoon phase, buddy." Which meant he didn't have full werewolf strength.

But…but Connor had told me that I had more strength. He said I threw a man across Eclipse after I did my rising-from-the-dead routine.

Of course, she didn't remember that particular act but…

Her hands fisted and she punched at Harris, as hard as she could.

He didn't fly across the room. He tried to look down at his now bleeding lip, then back up at her.

The knife —

His fingers locked around her neck. "Got you," he said.

No, no, not again. Please, no, not this.

His hands were tightening around her neck. He wasn't breaking her neck. He was choking her!

"Seriously, Harris," Connor roared, "I'm kicking your ass."

And, just like that, she was free because Connor had jerked Harris away from her. Connor spun the guy around to face him as Chloe fought to suck in some desperately needed air.

"You don't mess with her," Connor shouted. "You…*never* hurt her…" He drove his fist into the guy's face.

Harris's nose broke.

"He's…under a compulsion," Chloe managed to say. "I think…Keegan is controlling him…"

"That so?" Connor shoved the guy against the nearest wall and sank his teeth into Harris's throat. The move was so fast and so brutal that Chloe stood there, shocked.

This was different from when Connor drank from her. It was savage. Designed for pain. It was—

Connor pulled back and blood dripped down his chin. "Now I can control you." He glared at Harris. "*You never hurt, Chloe, understand? You protect her at all costs. You never hurt any of the Para Agents. We're on your side.*"

Harris's eyes still had that glassy look.

But he wasn't attacking, so that was good, right?

"Now come back to the land of the living," Connor snarled at him. "Shake Keegan's orders and get your ass in gear."

Harris shook his head. "C-Connor?"

Surprise rolled through Chloe.

"Well, I'll be damned," Connor said. "That shit worked." He glanced over at Chloe. "One compulsion can cancel out another." He swiped away the blood on his cheek. "Good to know." But she noticed that he didn't back away from Harris, not yet. "Are you in control?" Connor demanded of the other agent. "Or do I need to knock you out?"

Harris was tentatively touching his nose. And wincing. "I'm...in control. But I'm a little sketchy on how...I wound up here." His hand dropped and he glared at Connor. "You broke my nose, didn't you?"

Chloe cleared her throat. "He did that because you were trying to kill me."

Harris glanced at her. Horror flashed on his face. "I remember that! I'm so sorry!" Then his hands were running through his hair. "I hurt...I hurt a lot of people." Then his knees seemed to give way and he sank to the tiled floor. "Oh, God, what did I do?"

Connor stared down at him. "Not you, man. You were under a compulsion. It was Keegan. The bastard thought he could control you and that you'd do his dirty work for him." He looked over at Chloe. "He wanted you to kill her, but that wasn't happening."

She'd tucked the key card into her back pocket. Carefully, Chloe pushed it even deeper into that pocket.

Connor crossed to her side. His gaze swept over her. "Are you okay?"

"Yes. Fine." Should she tell him that she'd been running away? Make a big confession? Or keep that bit quiet?

"We need to find out what the hell other plans Keegan has in motion." Connor threaded his fingers with hers. "From here on out, I need you to stay with me."

Right. Staying together with the extra strong vampire-wolf sounded like a wonderful plan to her.

Harris pushed to his feet. "I...I lost the collar." He shook his head. "No, I convinced the other agents that...it was defective. Burning me too badly. They took it off." Fear flashed in his gaze. "I need something to control me! What if the beast comes out? What if—"

"It's several hours until the moon rises," Connor snapped. "If you get crazy before then, I'll deck you, okay?"

Harris nodded.

"Now let's get to the lab before Keegan springs any more surprises on us." His fingers tightened around Chloe's. Then he yanked her into his arms and just...held her. "Bastard thought he was going to take you from me. That *won't* happen."

She could feel the frantic beat of his heart against her. "I'm not going anywhere," she told him.

Chloe meant those words.

When she'd heard the screams behind her, she'd had one thought, just one.

Connor. Get to Connor. Make sure he's all right. Protect him.

She knew he was the big, bad alpha, but...he was also still hers. Hers to protect. Hers to love.

Even if he didn't love her back.

He squeezed her a moment longer. "Without you," he whispered, and she almost thought that she imagined those gruff words, "I'd be lost."

Then he pulled back. She blinked. Had he really just said—

But Connor was off at a run, and since he was still holding her hand, she had to run with him. They flew down the corridor, and Harris stumbled to keep up with them. The alarm was shrieking, hurting Chloe's ears, and as they turned and rushed down the hallway that would take them to Holly's lab, fear pushed through Chloe because she didn't know what she'd find in there. What if Keegan had managed to escape?

Connor shoved open the lab's doors.

For an instant, Chloe froze.

Keegan was strapped to a table. And Duncan...Duncan's fangs were bared. His claws were out. He was trying to go for Keegan's throat, but Holly was pulling her lover back, or, at least, she was trying to pull him back.

"*You're dead!*" Duncan yelled. "Dead! You're not my brother! You're nothing!"

And *that* had Chloe's mouth dropping open. Because...Duncan was Connor's brother. And if

Keegan was Duncan's brother... *No, no, no!* They couldn't be family!

A wave of unease had her shivering.

Keegan's head turned then. His eyes locked right on her. And she realized that he had eyes the exact shade as Duncan. But as she stared at him, she also noticed...

His chin...his chin has Connor's cleft.

His nose is like Duncan's, but his cheeks are like Connor's.

Like...Connor.

"Now all the family..." Keegan mumbled, "is together again."

Connor stared at Keegan, then Duncan.

"I would have...left him to die...too," Keegan said, his lips twisting. "Good thing...you saved...yourself, Duncan."

Duncan lurched forward.

"No!" Holly yelled. "Stop it! Can't you see? This is what he wants! He wants you to attack him! He wants you to be just as twisted on the inside as he is." She shook Duncan. "But you're not. You're nothing like him! You're nothing like your father! You are *mine*, Duncan. My lover. My life. So don't listen to him."

"Found you a...vampire to fuck...huh?" Keegan rasped. "That's what I did...too...Brothers just...alike. Fuck and...feed and ch-change..."

Duncan's whole body was tense, but he made no move to push past Holly.

"He's our brother?" Connor asked and his voice just sounded dead.

"So he says," Holly replied curtly. "But until we get the blood work back, nothing's for certain."

The twist in Chloe's gut told her it was certain. As she looked between the three men, she wondered how she hadn't seen the similarities before.

"Just how fucked up..." Connor said, "does one family really have to be?"

Before Keegan could speak again, Eric burst into the lab. "Stop them!" Eric yelled. "Stop them *now!*"

Chloe had no idea what he was talking about, but she figured the mess they were all in had just gotten worse.

Eric ran to Keegan. He grabbed the guy's jaw and jerked Keegan's head toward him. "You've put your entire pack under a compulsion, haven't you?"

"Figured it...would be a good idea." His voice sounded slurred to Chloe.

"They are *killing* themselves! The silver in their collars is turned up to full power and they're still fighting. They're clawing at the cell bars and burning."

Keegan laughed. A rough, choking sound.

"They're your pack! Are you seriously going to let them all die?"

Keegan was silent. Chloe found herself leaning forward, holding her breath, and then he said, "If I don't get what...I want...I'm going to let everyone...die."

Then his gaze slid to her. His face hardened. And she knew what he wanted.

CHAPTER THIRTEEN

"Kill him," Connor said flatly as he moved to stand in front of Chloe. Hell, no, he didn't like the way the guy was staring at Chloe. And Keegan was far too aware and chatty for his taste. Eric should have pumped him full of twice as many drugs. "The compulsion will end if you kill him." Seemed like the easiest plan to him.

Brother or no fucking brother.

Because if the guy was telling the truth, then, from what Connor had seen, Keegan had far more of their father's traits than anyone else. And dear old dad had been a sadistic bastard to the very end.

"Y-you don't have to kill him." Chloe's hand wrapped around Connor's arm. "Another vampire just needs to bite the werewolves. That vamp's compulsion can replace the one he gave to his pack."

Eric's head snapped up. "What?" Connor could practically see the wheels turning in his head. "Hell, yes, that could work."

"It *did* work on Harris," Chloe said.

Eric whirled for the door. "Shane can do it. No one can resist that guy's compulsion." Then he was racing away again.

Connor kept his position in front of Chloe. "My vote is still for killing Keegan now. Why take the chance and let him keep living?"

Chloe had been afraid the guy on the gurney would compel her. And what if he did? What if that jerk took control of Chloe's mind?

No one could hurt her. When Connor had found her and Harris together, hell, he'd nearly lost his control. And Harris had almost lost his head.

Holly glanced over at him. "There's more going on here than we realize." Connor noticed that she still hadn't let go of Duncan. Probably because she realized that the guy could attack at any moment. If he felt even half the rage that Connor did, then the temptation to kill Keegan had to be surging strong and hard through his veins.

Holly narrowed her eyes on Keegan. "How did you get a vampire to transform you?"

"Interesting thing…the vamp has to be female…only the female vamps can transfer the power…"

Connor's father had realized that, at the end. How had this guy learned the truth?

From someone at Purgatory? Did someone tip Keegan off? Had someone there been watching that

final battle with Connor, Duncan, and their father?
And that watcher had given the information to
Keegan?

"You think…the only prison…is Purgatory?"
Keegan's lips twisted but he lay docilely on the
table. "Senator Quick…he had a back-up. Not
dangerous paranormals there…weak ones. Easy
to control. To use. To…kill."

"No!" Horror sharpened Chloe's voice.
"That's not true!" She tried to run around Connor
and get to Keegan.

Connor caught her and held tight.

"True," Keegan whispered, his lips twisting.
"Started it…for you…because he wanted to make
you…stronger…so they died…for you."

Connor felt the tremble that slid over her
body. "No."

Keegan's smile stretched. "Can take you…to
them…you can…save them…"

She shook her head.

"If not…they die…tonight…by…midnight."

***

Eric ran back into containment. Shane was
standing near the cages, glaring at the men who
seemed determined to die.

"Fools," Shane muttered. "You're just
hurting—"

"Bite them!" Eric ordered.

Shane spun to face him. "Do what?"

"Bite them. Then compel them. Your compulsion will cancel out the order that Keegan bastard gave to them all." Because no one could resist one of Shane's compulsions. The guy was the most powerful vampire that Eric had ever encountered, and Shane was also the reason why Eric wasn't exactly human anymore.

"You're telling me to take werewolf blood," Shane said as his eyes widened a bit. "And with this many wolves, it's going to be a gorge fest."

Which meant Shane would get one serious power rush.

"Consider this your free pass."

Shane smiled. He flashed fang. And when the next werewolf shoved his hands against the silver bars, Shane just reached out, grabbed that hand, and sank his fangs into the guy's wrist.

One by one, Shane fed. He compelled. And soon, the men weren't enraged and on a crash course with death.

They were curled up on the floor. Sleeping.

Olivia ran into the room. "The guards are stable! And—um, Shane?"

He turned toward her. For an instant, even Eric thought about backing up because that guy looked damn scary.

"Shane?" Olivia said again as she edged closer to him. "What did you do?"

Gorged. "He saved their lives," Eric said.

And he had.

But now it looked like Shane might be on too much of a feeding high.

Olivia wrapped her arms around Shane. "Focus on me."

He shuddered, and his arms wrapped around her.

Mates…they could really do the damnedest things.

***

"He is their brother."

Their group — such as it was — had gathered in Eric's office.

The chaos was over. For the moment, anyway. Eric had told them all that the werewolves had been controlled, and Chloe hadn't asked a whole lot of questions about that control — especially once she'd gotten a look at Shane.

The vamp was in the office with them, but Olivia was keeping a close eye on him. And a hand. Chloe had noticed that Olivia was constantly touching her vamp. Trying to soothe him?

"I did a rush order on the blood work and DNA," Holly said, clearing her throat. "Had to use some of those special connections that Eric has…" She slanted a glance toward him. "But we hit a match. Keegan wasn't lying. I'm sorry to say it, Duncan and Connor, but Keegan really is your brother."

Chloe wanted to reach out to Connor. To touch him the way that Olivia touched the vamp, but Connor had marched away from her. He stood near a window, staring out as dusk swept over the area.

"He killed our mother's family." This news came from Duncan.

Connor's shoulders stiffened.

"He said...he said they blamed him. That they saw our father in him, and he killed them all."

"I see our father in him," Connor said. "He's just as eaten up with hate and evil as our old man ever was."

Eric was behind his desk. His gaze slid from Duncan to Connor...then to Chloe. Eric exhaled and said, "I think he may be telling the truth about another prison facility."

Chloe shook her head.

"Someone had to transform him," Eric continued roughly. "And from my own intel work, I can tell you that I'd already begun to suspect that the senator had taken some not-so-willing volunteers for his experiments. I'd actually thought he was trying to experiment in Purgatory, but my men found no evidence of that. When Case Killian was working undercover as the warden, he had a full run of the prison, and he never saw any experiments." He shook his head. "No, the senator was doing those somewhere else. Somewhere that he could monitor. And I believe that he *was* using weaker prey."

"The better to control and to kill," Connor muttered.

Eric nodded. Chloe didn't think Connor saw that faint movement.

Her heart seemed to be encased in ice. Those people—they could be suffering or dying right at that moment.

No, no, he said they had until midnight.

"I doubt they're criminals," Eric continued. "Probably just unlucky bastards that the senator found and imprisoned. Victims that he didn't think anyone would miss."

Her father had been such a stellar human being. Shame wrapped heavily around her. "*We* have to find them," Chloe said.

All eyes turned to her—including Connor's glittering stare.

"If they're out there, we have to help them."

"The only person who knows their location is Keegan," Eric said, his jaw locking. "Shane checked with the other prisoners, he compelled them...but they don't know where the place is."

"Then we can compel Keegan! We can make him—"

Connor shook his head. "It doesn't work that way. You can't compel...someone...something like us."

Connor wasn't a thing. He was *her* lover. Her mate.

Her shoulders straightened. "Keegan said he would take us to them."

"No," Holly's voice was soft. "He said he would take *you* to them, Chloe."

She nodded. "Then let's do it."

And they were all back to looking at her like she was crazy. So maybe she was. After everything that had happened, how could she not be?

"We can't leave them. We have no idea what's being done to them. What if Keegan left orders for someone to make a paranormal army? What if my father did?" Because that crap would be right up his alley. "This started with me, and it needs to end with me." So many lives wasted, and why? For her?

I'm not worthy of anyone else dying.

"You're not a Para Agent," Eric pointed out.

Uh, yes, she was aware of that fact. No shiny badge for her.

"And I'm not just going to let a powerhouse like Keegan waltz through the doors of this base and head out into the sunset."

And the sun was setting. The full moon would be out soon. She could feel it calling to her.

"Then what are you going to do?" Chloe wanted to know. "Ship him off to Purgatory? Keep him in isolation there? Hope he never breaks free and drinks from all the werewolves there? Compels them—"

"I'm working on a game plan," Eric said.

Right. "In the meantime, I have a plan." After years of being afraid and hiding, it was time for her to do something. "I'm the unkillable woman."

She saw Eric's eyelids flicker.

Connor took a step toward her.

"What's the worst that can happen to me? I mean, I go in with Keegan and he kills me again. So, what?" Her gaze slid to Olivia. "I'll just come back."

Olivia had paled—and she was a vamp now, so she'd been a little pale to begin with. "But what if you don't?" Olivia asked. "My wishes…they were messed up, Chloe."

"You wanted me to always come back," she reminded her.

"But that doesn't mean you *will* always come back the same!" Olivia fired back. "Who knows what could happen to you! You can't just—"

"I'm like a cat with nine lives." She lifted her chin and glanced back over at Eric. "Come on, if I were one of your agents, you know you'd use me."

"The fuck he would," Connor snapped and he stalked toward her.

But Eric nodded and looked thoughtful. "I would."

"Then send me out. Connor and Duncan are the two who can defeat him in a fight, right? Send them as back-up, just like you did at Eclipse. If anything goes wrong, they can attack with fangs bared and claws at the ready." Her words were coming a little too fast. She needed to slow them down and also slow down her racing heartbeat.

Connor stood in front of her now. A furrow had appeared between his brows. "Why are you saying this? There's no way Eric is going to let you walk out with a killer!"

Actually, she thought Eric was considering it.

Connor's hands curled around her shoulders. "Why?"

"Because it's not about me. It's not about me running and protecting myself." What she'd always planned. To run. To disappear. To leave everything else behind.

Selfish.

"Those people out there…if they were imprisoned because of me, then I owe them. I have to try and help them."

"Even if you die?" Connor asked.

She smiled at him. "I come back." *I'll always come back for you.*

Being with Connor had made her realize something important. She wasn't alone. There were others out there that she could depend on, others who could depend on her. With the Para Agents in that room, Chloe actually felt as if she belonged. She hadn't belonged anywhere, not really, in a very long time.

I belong with Connor. And she needed to prove herself. To Connor. To them all. To show them that she could be more than the woman who tried to escape.

She could be the woman who fought.

"No." Connor shook his head. "No, you can't be put at risk like this. *No.*"

"Yes," Eric said in the same instant.

And Connor rushed across that room toward Eric. His hands slapped onto Eric's desk. "I'm done. No more jobs for you. Nothing. You want to throw my ass back in Purgatory? Then go ahead." He gave a grim shake of his head. "But I'm not working for you. I'm not going to let you risk Chloe. I'm taking her out of here. That's what she wanted from the beginning, and I should have listened to her. I should have put Chloe first because she is the one who matters most to me."

Chloe couldn't breathe.

"Her protection, her safety, will always come first. She is mine, and I am damn well hers."

She had to blink away tears. Connor was so sexy to her right then.

Even though his claws were digging into Eric's desk, he was just hot.

Then Connor spun toward her. He marched back to Chloe's side, and he offered her a claw-tipped hand. "Let's get the hell out of here." His gaze held hers. "Any place you want to go. No one will know your past and we'll make the future anything you want it to be."

She wanted to take his hand. "I love you." She was certain of it. The wild tumble of emotion she felt for Connor had to be love.

His eyes widened.

"But I can't go with you. If Keegan is telling the truth, and those people die—"

"They're paranormals," Eric pointed out. "Not just people—"

"Same thing," Chloe said flatly.

"Yes…" Eric murmured.

"I can't live with that on me." Okay, technically, she could pretty much keep living through everything. "I need to help them. It's not just about me."

"Baby." Connor's hand cupped her cheek. His claws never so much as scratched her. "I just want you safe."

"And I will be safe because you will be there with me every step of the way. You and Duncan are stronger than he is. I know you are." She trusted him completely. "You'll have my back."

"Always," he whispered as his head lowered toward hers. "But don't do this…don't take this risk. We can leave. I want to go with you. Before,

I wanted to go with you when we were upstairs. *I want you*."

She kissed him. Right there. So what if everyone was watching. Her hands slid over the hard line of his jaw and she rose up against him. "I want you more than anything," she said, meaning those words with every fiber of her being. "We'll help these people. We'll win, and then we can be together. We can look to the future." Because she wanted her future to be with him. Whatever came her way, it would be with him.

His eyes closed. "I can't deny you."

Her heart raced faster.

"I wish I could." His eyes opened and they were glowing with power. "If Keegan makes one wrong move, he's a dead man."

Yes! He was going to help her. Chloe threw her arms around Connor and hugged him tight.

He lifted her up against him and held her, so close. *So close.*

Over Connor's shoulder, she saw Eric watching them. His head had cocked and his gaze had turned calculating.

Uh, oh.

"Before this mission," Eric murmured, "Connor, I'll need a word alone with you."

Chloe pulled back. She shook her head —

"Only a moment," Eric said and he smiled. That smile didn't reach his eyes. "I have to make sure that Connor fully understands the mission."

It was a recovery mission. What more was there to understand? Even she got that.

But the others were filing out of the office.

"You'll all be briefed soon," Eric promised as he rose from his desk. "Every precaution will be taken. Every single one."

Connor squeezed Chloe's hand. "Wait for me in the courtyard."

She nodded. Her gaze searched his a moment more, then she slid from the room. When the door closed behind her, Chloe clenched her hands into fists. She looked up and found Olivia staring at her.

"Are you sure about this?" Olivia asked her, worry darkening her eyes.

"Yes." It had to be done. And she wasn't going to just hide in the shadows and wait for someone else to save the day. She tried to smile. "Are you sure you don't have another wish in you? Maybe one that makes me indestructible and lets me live forever with the man I love?"

Olivia hesitated. "I wish I could do that for you..."

Chill bumps rose on Chloe's arms. Olivia had just used the big W word.

Olivia hugged her. "Be safe, my friend."

***

"So…you're done with the Para Unit, huh?"

Connor glared at Eric. "If Chloe is going on this mission, I'll be at her back. But after this…yeah, the slate was supposed to be clean, remember? Chloe was my last case."

"She's more than a case, isn't she?" Eric opened his laptop and flipped it around to face Connor.

What was the guy planning?

Eric tapped on a few of the keys.

"You're willing to give up everything for her, aren't you?"

Yes.

He'd realized that fact when he'd seen her fighting with Harris.

"What do you think she'd give up for you?"

His chin lifted as Connor crossed his arms over his chest. "It doesn't matter." She'd said she loved him. With every bit of his tattered heart, he wanted that to be true. But with all the sins on him, hell, why would she love someone like him? Chloe was good. She was risking her life for people she didn't even know. She was—

"I've got something for you to see," Eric muttered. He tapped on the keyboard once more.

Chloe's image appeared on the screen.

"This is from my security cameras. It was taken earlier, you know, before all hell broke loose." Eric sat on the edge of the desk. "That right there...of course, is Chloe."

Connor growled.

"She's got a key card. Tricky little wolf. I didn't even see her swipe it from my office." He paused and glanced around. "Huh, wonder if she took anything this time?"

Connor leaned toward that small screen. "She's...leaving." *Leaving me. Because I said I wouldn't go with her.* He knew this had been right after Chloe told him that she could love him...*and I didn't say a damn word back to her.*

"See...right there...she only has one more door and she's free. Watch it, watch — yes, that door is opening now."

Freedom was right in front of her.

"This is when the screaming starts."

He saw Chloe whirl around.

Eric paused the video.

"She could've left then. Just headed out into the night and vanished. We sure had our hands full. It would have been a while before we could search for her."

Connor shook his head.

"But watch this..." Eric hit the button to play the video once more. The camera had a perfect shot of Chloe's face and the fear in her expression stole Connor's breath. So much fear and —

"Ah, did you see it? She said something." Eric rewound the video. "Let's watch again."

And he could see it. Perfectly. It looked as if Chloe was yelling something.

Connor!

He rubbed a hand over his chest.

"She was free and clear to leave. But she ran right back into hell for one reason," Eric said.

When Connor looked over at Eric, he saw that the other man wasn't watching the video. Instead, Eric was staring straight at Connor.

"Now you know what she'd do for you." Eric's gaze swept over Connor. "The question is…what would you do for her?"

"Anything," he promised.

Eric smiled. "I was hoping you'd say that."

CHAPTER FOURTEEN

The night truly was beautiful.

Chloe stared up at the stars. Bright and glittering. She didn't see the moon, not yet, but she could feel it. A starry, moon-filled night.

Her arms wrapped around her stomach as she stood there. She didn't like the silence. It was giving her too much time to think and to fear. To wonder...what if?

What if I die and don't come back?

What if this is my last night with Connor?

What if we don't have a chance at forever?

What if this moment is all we have?

The door opened behind her. She looked over her shoulder and saw Connor. His eyes gleamed in the darkness.

She turned toward him. Opened her arms. Tipped back her head.

When he kissed her, the *what if's* in her mind finally quieted. She drank him in, loving his touch, needing him so much that her whole body ached.

So this is love.

She'd always wondered what it would be like. For some reason, she'd thought it would be sweeter. Softer. Kind of like a sappy song on the radio.

She hadn't known it would be so hot and wild and consuming. She hadn't known that it would twist her up in knots. That it would wreck her.

That it would make her stronger.

It had.

"We don't have much time," Connor said. "Baby, I need to be with you...please, let me have you again. Right here."

She wanted to be with him a thousand more times.

"Here, now...with the stars on you. No one else can see. It's just us. Baby, always us."

He lifted her into his arms. Carried her back to the side of the building. They were hidden there, behind the door. He stripped her. His touch tender, his desire obvious in the fire that lit his gaze.

Her hands weren't as tender on him. She was frantic to feel him. She shoved up his shirt. Her hands slid over his hot, muscled flesh. Then she moved down, down, and opened the button of his jeans.

He was strong. He positioned her, held her easily, and her legs curled around him. One thrust—and he sank to the hilt inside of her. She was so full that Chloe felt stretched and it was amazing. She loved the way he filled her. When he withdrew and thrust in again, her eyes nearly rolled back in her head. He was holding her, surrounding her so totally, consuming and dominating as he controlled the rhythm. The guy was driving her out of her head.

Chloe's nails bit into his back. She offered him her neck. "Bite me." Because she knew just how to push them both over the edge.

His breath blew over her neck. Hot. Making her tremble.

Then his fangs sank into her.

Pleasure ripped through Chloe and her body went bow-tight. Her right hand flew out. She grabbed the fence, not even thinking about the silver until it was too late —

But it didn't burn.

He thrust deep.

Her sex clamped around him, holding so tight.

She rose up, pushed back against him, and his teeth stayed in her neck. Pleasure hit her, rolling through her again and again and Chloe cried out, unable to stop herself because it was too much.

Her sex contracted around him as the orgasm blasted through her. She couldn't breathe, for a moment, she wasn't even sure if she could see.

The pleasure was so intense it was almost painful. Almost...

"Connor!"

He poured into her. He shuddered and held her so tight. She wanted to freeze that moment. To hold it close because as he lifted his head and looked at her, Chloe could have sworn that she saw emotion—love—flash in his eyes.

I want him to love me. I want him to feel just a little bit of the emotion that I feel for him. I want —

The pleasure crested again.

He held her close.

Her legs were trembling when the waves of release finally ended. Ever so carefully, Connor righted her clothes. He brushed back her hair. He kissed her cheek.

Then he yanked his jeans back into position.

Chloe stared at him. Her heart was still racing in a triple-time beat. "He's...he's going to know what we just did." She should have thought of that before. Keegan would catch the scent, he'd know—

"Fuck what he knows. You're mine, and the whole world needs to recognize that fact."

She was his. And he was hers.

He stood before her. So strong and powerful. Brave.

"I'm scared, Chloe," Connor confessed.

She shook her head, sure that she'd misheard. Not Connor. Not—

"You're the one thing I can't lose," he said.

"You won't lose me."

He swallowed. "What I'm about to do...if there was another choice, I wouldn't...I wouldn't do it."

Okay, those words were *not* good. Some of her bright post-sex and post-multiple orgasm glow began to fade.

"If something happens, if Keegan bites you, he *will* compel you."

Her worst fear.

"Today, we learned that another compulsion can cancel out his power."

Yes, right, but that compulsion had been given *after* Keegan's.

"Eric wants me to try something with you." His breath exhaled on a ragged sigh. "He wants me to compel you, and baby, I think I should. I just...I *can't* do it without telling you first."

He'd better not tell her to forget the mission. Or to forget him. Or to—

"I want to compel you...to ignore any suggestions or orders that Keegan gives you. Hell, this shit might not work, it's just a shot in the dark. But Eric and I think that *any* additional chance we have—"

She threw her arms around him. "Do it."

"Chloe?"

She looked up at him. "Compel me. I don't want to be used against you or the other agents. I want to help. I want to be strong."

"Baby, you are strong."

She tried to smile for him.

He kissed her once more. Such a soft, gentle kiss.

Then Connor looked into her eyes. The stars behind him didn't seem to shine as bright. They turned a little hazy, but his voice was so clear…

"Chloe, you will not let Keegan into your mind. You will not let him control you. He will not compel you to follow any orders. If he tries you will only hear my voice…"

His voice was all she could hear right then.

"You will hear my voice, Chloe, and you will resist him. You will hear my voice, and you will ignore him. You will hear my voice…"

She waited, her body locked down…

"And you will know how much I fucking love you."

***

"Another armored van?" Keegan murmured when he was led inside—and then shackled in place. "How not surprising."

Connor kept his gun ready and aimed at the bastard. One wrong move, and he'd pump the guy full of so many drugs that Keegan would be drooling on the floorboard.

Beside him, Duncan was armed, too. Duncan was on his left. And Chloe was on his right.

The back door swung closed and Connor heard the distinct sound of Eric locking that door as he secured them inside.

A small window was overhead. One that let the moonlight spill into the transport van.

Keegan stretched a bit, as if trying to reach for that light. Then he sighed and glanced over at Chloe. "You screwed him again. I hate it when you wear his stench."

Connor's finger tightened on the trigger.

Chloe patted his leg. But she told Keegan, "Start giving us directions."

That had been the deal. Keegan was conscious because he had to give them directions to his little house of horrors. His voice wasn't slurred because Eric had eased off on the guy's dosage.

A bad idea.

Keegan looked up at the window. "We'd better hurry. At midnight, everything will end."

Chloe pulled out her radio.

"We'll drive down the main road here…for about forty-minutes. Then head west."

Chloe relayed those instructions.

"I'll give you more directions as we go,"
Keegan said. "Wouldn't want to give too much
away, too soon."

Connor really wanted to shoot the guy.

The truck lurched forward.

Silence.

"Bet you and Duncan didn't even know
about me...I mean I did my research on you two.
You were so young, it makes sense you didn't
remember me. And Duncan?" His laughter was
low. "He was so fucked up after our father killed
our mom...hell, he didn't remember much of
anything did he?"

Connor just stared at the bastard. But, yes,
the guy was right. Connor didn't recall a damn
thing about him and as for Duncan...*Duncan
didn't even know me when we first met.*

"Do you remember our mother dying?"
Keegan asked. "I've always been curious about
that."

Connor could hear the echo of screams in his
mind.

"Are the stories I've heard true? You and
Duncan were supposed to stay in the closet, but
you ran out?"

He'd been so young. A lost kid. Afraid of the
dark.

"Did she die protecting you?"

Connor's chin lifted. Chloe's shoulder brushed against his. "Yes," he said flatly. "She loved me." He'd always clung to that one truth.

Keegan looked back up at the window. "What a fucking waste." Silence. "All her family? Guess why they died?"

Connor didn't want to guess.

"Because they didn't love me," Keegan murmured.

Duncan shot off the bench.

Connor grabbed him before Duncan could take Keegan's head.

Keegan laughed. "This is going to be such a fun night. I've got so many surprises planned."

***

Eric stared at the screen in front of him. "I'll just bet you do."

Chloe didn't have to radio the directions back to him. That whole armored van was wired for sound and video. But Keegan didn't know that…and anything that bastard didn't know…

Gives us an advantage.

"All right, people," he said to the group in *his* van. "We're looking at a destination we can access by midnight. As we keep driving, we'll work to narrow this shit down. We want to know the location as soon as we can. The last thing we want is to send our agents in there blind." The sooner they knew the location, the sooner he could get an air patrol in to sweep the area.

His gaze stayed locked on the monitor. Keegan should be secured, for the time being.

But worry still gnawed at him because he'd learned long ago...when it came to paranormals...*should* didn't apply.

***

"We're nearing Wessex Road," Keegan murmured after they'd driven and driven for at least two hours, following his sketchy directions. "Turn right on Wessex."

Connor heard Chloe speak those same directions into her radio.

"Ah, Chloe..." Keegan shook his head and pulled lightly on his restraints. "I have to confess, I thought you'd be too afraid to come on this particular mission."

"I'm not afraid of you," she said, voice flat.

"Liar," Keegan accused. "Ever since Eclipse, I bet I've been starring in your nightmares." He licked his lips and studied her. "Though you did surprise me there. I was so enraged that you'd screwed Connor, my emotions got a little out of control."

"I didn't just have sex with him," Chloe said, still in that calm, unemotional voice. "I mated him."

Rage twisted Keegan's face—just for an instant. "Mating isn't really for life. It's just until one of you dies. But, in your case, death doesn't take, does it, sweetheart?"

"I'm not your sweetheart."

Keegan leaned forward, as much as his restraints would allow. "You were supposed to be. Your father promised you to me. A perfect virgin werewolf…easy for breeding. He even adjusted your scent so that I'd be pulled in…every time I smelled you, it was like I'd caught a bit of paradise."

"I can't even shift," Chloe said. "Why waste your time with me?"

Keegan shook his head. "Now see, that's where your thinking was wrong. Your father's was wrong, too. He thought you had to go full-on wolf to be strong, but you're better than that. You have the beast's power, but it never fully controls you. You don't have to worry about losing yourself to the beast." He smiled at her. "You see flaws. When I look at you, I see perfection."

It was taking all of Connor's control not to leap off that bench.

"Does he see perfection?" Keegan asked and he inclined his head toward Connor. "Have you asked him just what he sees when he looks at you? Because I think his answer might surprise you."

Connor felt Chloe's gaze cut to him, but she didn't speak.

If she had asked, he would have told her the truth. *I see my life. My future. Every wish I've ever had.*

"When I get stuck between shifts," Chloe said, "is that still perfection?"

"Ah...those happened because of your father. He was messing with you. Trying to draw out the full wolf. I changed your injections back to normal for the last year."

Connor felt surprise ripple through Chloe.

"Your claws came out, your teeth sharpened, and your enhanced strength was there. All without the pesky problem of being a full-on werewolf."

Chloe shook her head. "No, those shifts that didn't work, the pain—"

"That was all on your father. Twisted bastard. He should have just accepted perfection when he had it."

She trembled near Connor.

"I'm sorry I killed you," Keegan told Chloe. The jerk's voice actually sounded almost sincere. What a lie. "But...it certainly opened some new doors, didn't it? I thought you were good before...and now...oh, now, sweetheart, I'll do anything to have you."

Those words sounded like a warning.

It was time for Connor to give his own warning. "And I'd do *anything* to protect her from you."

Keegan slanted a fast glance Connor's way. "Would you kill for her?"

"Yes," he gritted out.

"Turn on your friends? Your own brother?"

Fuck it. "Yes."

"Would you die for her?" Keegan taunted.

"Connor, stop," Chloe said.

"Yes," he told Keegan. "Anything."

Keegan inclined his head. "Good. You just might get the chance to prove that."

Silence.

The miles ticked past. The moon rose higher. Its power called to Connor.

"I saw you when you were a child, Connor." Keegan's voice had gone cold. "I found you…right after I turned eighteen. You were younger, probably, what…twelve? You hadn't shifted yet. I could tell because when I watched our father peel the skin off your chest, you didn't heal."

"You sonofabitch," Duncan snarled.

"I watched that for a long time. It was interesting. You didn't cry out for mercy. You didn't beg. You just…endured."

Duncan lifted his gun. "Shut up."

"I realized then that you were really more like our mother. You didn't fight back. You just took the pain he gave you." Keegan shook his head. "And I was like our father...because then I went home and I tore the flesh from those bastards who'd raised me. They begged for mercy, but I didn't give them any."

Duncan's gun fired.

The dart didn't hit Keegan, but it lodged into the side of the van, less than an inch from Keegan's head.

"I won't miss next time," Duncan promised.

Connor realized his own claws had come out.

"Turn left on Geronimo," Keegan said.

And Chloe sucked in a sharp breath.

"Oh, starting to figure this out, are you?" Keegan asked her. "It took you long enough."

***

"There is no Geronimo Road or Geronimo Street or Geronimo Avenue on the map," Olivia said, sounding frustrated. "The guy is just jerking us around."

Eric didn't think so. He'd caught the sound of Chloe's quickly indrawn breath.

Then he heard the crackle of her radio coming to life.

"In about thirty minutes, we'll be coming to an old dirt road," Chloe said. "It doesn't have a real name...I used to call it Geronimo Lane. My...my mother and I called it that. She was part

Apache, and she used to tell me stories about Geronimo." Her words came a little faster. "She had an old ranch up here. We'd ride horses in the summer. I thought my dad had sold the place after she died. He never let me come back here."

Probably because he turned the place into his own experimental prison.

Olivia was pulling up a larger map of the area on her laptop. He saw a big building, one that looked to be surrounded by a heavy fence.

Metal or silver? He'd lay odds on silver.

"We've got a destination," he muttered to the team with him. "Now let's move the hell in. And be ready — for *anything*."

CHAPTER FIFTEEN

"Have you ever wondered about your mother?" Keegan asked Chloe.

They were driving down Geronimo Lane. She could hear the echo of laughter around her. Feel the memories. She'd been so happy there. Riding on the horse with her mom. Her hair had flown behind her and they'd gone so fast.

"She left your father for another man, but come on...did you blame her?"

No, she hadn't.

I just wished that she'd taken me with her.

"You know, that story was bullshit. She didn't leave with another man."

Her fingers tightened around the radio.

"She was like you, Chloe. A werewolf. She realized your father wasn't...well, he wasn't her type."

Did she realize he was crazy?

"She was going to take you both away, but he stopped her."

The van slowed. Braked.

"And he brought her here. I think she was his very first prisoner."

The back doors opened. Chloe ran and jumped out, nearly hitting Eric. She spun around and saw a big, gleaming fence circling the property. Silver? Yes, yes, it looked silver.

Is my mother in there? That couldn't be possible.

She walked toward the fence. Once upon a time, a small ranch house had stood about thirty yards away. Now, a tall, menacing building rose from the darkness.

"This is the original Purgatory," Keegan said. "Only there are just a few prisoners left here now."

"Lock him in the vehicle," Eric ordered as Duncan and Connor climbed out of the van. "We'll go into this place and find out what the hell is happening."

Chloe's feet felt rooted to the spot.

"If he's got prisoners in there, then he probably compelled them," Duncan warned. "We need to fire the tranqs on sight. Let's knock them all out, then we can assess things."

Shoot first? But—

"Is it midnight yet?" Keegan asked, sounding mildly curious. "It sure feels close to the witching hour." His voice deepened. "You didn't catch all of my pack, you know. I had a few waiting in the wings. Waiting here. Waiting…until they saw us arrive."

An explosion rocked the night. The force of the blast sent Chloe flying back. Before she hit the ground, Connor caught her and held tight.

She looked up and saw the fire blazing, just behind the fence. Rising and rising, the orange and gold flames were shooting toward the sky.

"Better hurry, if you want to save anyone…" Keegan said.

Then she heard the cries. Howls and screams. And they were all coming from the fire.

"Oh, my God." She glanced into the armored van, staring at Keegan in horror. "What did you do?"

"I said I'd take you to them…"

Eric and Connor were running toward the fence.

"I never said anyone would get out of that place alive."

She started running after Connor. Keegan's mocking laughter followed her.

***

"Do you want your brother to die?" Keegan asked Duncan.

Duncan had taken a position at the back of the armored van. Duncan still had that gun of his at the ready.

"I mean…your other brother. Connor. Not me." Keegan smiled. "Because Connor needs back-up. I might have left some seriously fucked-up inmates waiting on him."

Over Duncan's shoulder, he saw the doctor—Holly—rushing after Connor.

"And there goes your vamp mate," he added. "A tasty little morsel. They'll eat her right up."

"Holly can handle herself," Duncan growled.

But he looked over his shoulder.

"Normally, she could. She can't…not against what's waiting inside." Time for a new surprise. "I lied…I do that. There aren't innocents inside. No one is innocent any longer. They're the monsters we made—the senator and I." That dumbass David Vincent had never ever realized how much Keegan and the senator had been scheming together. Even if the guy hadn't lost his wolf, Keegan had planned to take over as pack alpha. "We played and now they wait." He could smell the smoke. "It's really better to let them all burn. I'm doing you a favor with the fire. Because if they get out, they'll kill anything in their path." He exhaled. "It's such a good thing that my Chloe can come back from death." He paused. "Can your Holly?"

"Screw you," Duncan said. Then he fired a tranq dart. The dart came at Keegan, spinning, fast—

He doubled-over. Sagged and hit the bottom of that van.

"Keep an eye on him!" Keegan heard Duncan shout. "Don't let him out of your sight. If he so much as twitches, shoot him again."

Then Duncan was running away.

Ah, that was the way of mates. If one was in danger, the other had to rush in to the rescue.

He uncurled his claws. Being a cross-over did have its benefits.

He'd just fucking caught that tranq with his claws. Caught it and...

"Hey, asshole..." Keegan called to the man standing guard. "I'm twitching."

The guard—a human—raised his weapon.

Keegan threw the dart at him. It hit the guy in the chest and the man fell back, crying out. But Keegan was already tearing at his shackles. He broke his wrists and he got his hands free. Cracked his ankles and escaped.

When he leapt from the back of that armored van, he was already transforming. He bounded out, moving fast, faster...

Duncan leapt into his path.

Hello, brother. I get to kill you first.

***

Eric beat her to the door. He ripped it right off its hinges, just yanked that heavy metal door out of the way as if it weighed nothing.

Someone has been holding back on us.

Smoke billowed out, choking her, and Chloe put her hands over her mouth. She and Connor ran inside and—

A werewolf leapt at Connor. The beast came out, with his teeth going right for Connor's throat. Connor grabbed the wolf and slung him back.

"Stop!" Chloe screamed at the wolf. "We're trying to help you!"

The werewolf charged at her. It rushed, moving faster and faster, and its eyes were wild.

She lifted her gun and fired. The tranq hit the werewolf in the side.

"Shoot first," Chloe whispered. Right. Okay. She could see where that might be a good idea in this place.

Because it was *chaos.*

Eric grabbed the wolf Chloe had just hit and dragged him from the inferno. She saw Holly pull another unconscious wolf outside.

Chloe turned to the right and nearly ran into Connor. He wasn't moving. Just staring at her with a glittering gaze.

"Connor?"

"We need to get out."

"There are more—" Chloe coughed on the smoke. "More people here…we can help! They're panicking because of the fire."

Then she heard the low, menacing growls.

Through the smoke, she saw the increasing glow of the silver eyes.

"No," Connor said. "They're attacking because that's what Keegan wants them to do."

Connor raised his gun. Her fingers tightened on her weapon. They both fired when the werewolves—at least five of them—attacked.

***

Duncan had Keegan on the ground. Keegan could feel the press of the bastard's claws on his throat.

He could also hear the thunder of gunfire.

"How long…will their tranqs last?" He knew how to play this jerk. "Are you going to…leave your brother again? Let him scream? Beg?"

Duncan's gaze shot to the right. Toward the sound of that gunfire.

"Die?" Keegan taunted.

Duncan's claws cut into Keegan's throat.

"Maybe you are like our father…"

"Duncan!"

Fuck, now who was it?

But then he caught the scents in the air—the blonde vampire and his mate.

"Duncan, get in there and help Connor! We'll control Keegan."

They wished they could.

But Duncan was on his feet. And running for the house.

Keegan stayed on the ground, biding his time. Yes, the vampire was supposed to be strong. He'd researched this one. And the woman with him...he knew she was the one who'd killed David Vincent's beast. "I should thank you," he said to her.

The flames were crackling.

"Because of you, I got to be alpha. David was in my way for so long." He nodded. "So I'll let you live."

She glared down at him.

"Don't have a wish for me?" he taunted her. "Because I thought that was what you did. You made wishes come true."

"Not anymore," she told him. Ah, yes, *there* was a flash of fang.

How disappointing. Now she was just another vamp.

"You should have been more." He turned his head, but made no move to leap to his feet. "Perhaps you could have saved them then."

Because it was only a matter of time. He hadn't just planned one explosion...

That building will burn to the ground.

Time for more fireworks.

***

Another explosion shook the building. Connor grabbed Chloe and held her tight, covering her with his body as chunks of the ceiling rained down on him. "We have to get out!" They'd already dragged out the werewolves who'd attacked them. "Come on, we need to go!"

Chloe was covered in ash and she trembled against him.

Screw this shit. It had obviously been a set-up from the beginning. He lifted Chloe into his arms and ran for the door —

"*Help me!*"

The words reached him as a whisper. So low. So lost.

A woman's voice.

He stilled.

"Connor? Connor, what is it?"

He looked over his shoulder. More fire was spreading. More explosions. The place had been set so that it would destroy them when they raced inside.

And it would destroy the paranormals Keegan and the senator had kept here.

One of those paranormals sounded as if she were trapped below. And she was begging for help.

"Connor?"

He carried Chloe outside. The fire was too hot. Burning too bright.

He saw Duncan rushing toward him. Saw Holly just a few steps away. Eric was kneeling near the unconscious pile of werewolves.

Connor's breath burned in his lungs.

"Help me!" That desperate voice wouldn't be heard by everyone. No, it—

"Connor, someone is in there!" Chloe's enhanced senses had picked up the cry. "Someone is trapped!"

Or someone *was* a trap. He pressed a kiss to her lips. "I've got her." And he nodded to Eric as he put Chloe down away from the fire.

I know what I'll do for Chloe. Everything.

"Connor, wait, no, I'm the one who doesn't stay dead!" She lunged after him. "Connor!"

He ran back into the fire.

When he looked back, he saw that Eric had wrapped his arms around Chloe and was holding her tight. She was struggling in Eric's hold, but Eric held tightly to her.

She wouldn't rush after him, but Connor *would* be coming back to her.

"Connor!"

***

Keegan stretched lightly on the ground. "It's a pity," he said, shaking his head. "That you're both just vampires now…"

The other agents had been scouting the woods, but they hadn't found his men. Not yet.

"Pity," he said again.

His men—his werewolves—would have heard his voice right then. They would know… *Vampires*…

The shots rang out. Shane tried to jump in front of Olivia. He took the bullets meant for her. As he watched, Keegan knew at least one of the bullets slammed into Shane's heart.

And, just like that, he went down, frozen. As still as the dead.

More wooden bullets flew, but Keegan didn't wait to see if they were hitting Olivia. He was running and shifting. Before this night was done, he would kill his brothers. He would have Chloe. He would have all the power that was his due. The moon shone down on him, and the beast inside of him clawed for his freedom.

***

"Gunfire!" Eric shouted. "Agents, watch your backs!"

And his hold eased on Chloe. That little slip was all she needed. She lunged out of his arms and ran toward the building and the fire.

"Help me!"

She could hear that call. Coming from downstairs. She rushed inside and tried to stay as low as she could. Just because she came back from death, that didn't mean that she wanted to actually die again. She wanted —

"Hello, sweetheart."

Hard hands grabbed her and yanked Chloe up against Keegan.

"So much smoke…they didn't see me come in…I'm too fast for them."

And he was strong. Too strong. As if he'd never been drugged at all.

"Let's have that taste. I'll *make* you like it."

His teeth sank into her throat. And, damn him, he was making his bite pleasurable. That drugging, addictive pleasure that could come from a vampire's bite. She tried to fight him, punching and clawing, but he kept drinking her blood. Taking and taking…

No! Stop!

He wasn't.

And she…she couldn't even cry out.

That's part of a vampire's power. He makes you want the bite. Makes you want it more than anything else.

But she didn't want his bite. She didn't want him. She wanted Connor.

"Now…" Keegan lifted his head and stared into her eyes. "Aren't you delicious?"

She couldn't move.

"I want you to scream for me, Chloe. Scream for Connor…"

No, she wouldn't listen to his compulsion. She wouldn't…

Connor!

***

The stairs were burning. The fire had licked over his arm and the side of his face. Connor burst into the basement, his gaze frantically flying to the left and the right.

He saw the woman, huddled on the ground. The fire hadn't reached her, not yet.

When he took a step toward her, her head whipped up, and she bared her fangs at him.

Vampire.

Long chains circled her wrists and ankles.

She was so thin, her hair tumbled down her back in lank tangles, and her eyes reflected hell.

She's the reason Keegan is a cross-over.

"I'm here to help you," Connor told her as he advanced on her slowly. A vampire would normally be able to break free of chains like that, no problem, but the woman before him looked as if she'd been starved. How long had it been since she'd had blood?

"Wolf…wolf…just like him." The woman shook her head. "Not help, *hurt.*"

"Yeah, well, I might look a little like the bastard, but I'm not him." He broke the manacle that circled her right wrist. Shattered the manacle that bound her left wrist. "And you can—"

She rushed away from him, running up the stairs faster than he could blink.

"Thank me later," Connor muttered. He hefted the chains in his arms. He held them and—

"*Connor!*"

Chloe's voice. But Chloe shouldn't be in the building. Eric had her outside. Eric would be keeping her safe.

Still holding those chains, he ran for the stairs. He climbed them even as fire rolled across the walls. Then he was back on the main level of the building.

"She's mine, *brother*."

And Chloe was there. So was Keegan.

Her neck was bleeding. Fire was all around her. And Keegan was behind her.

"Chloe is mine now. She'll do anything for me. Always...*me*." Keegan's claws were at her throat.

"Chloe, baby, are you okay?" He could swing those chains and hit Keegan. Maybe that would free Chloe and she could run out of the inferno.

"Tell him that you're mine, Chloe," Keegan ordered.

Chloe's gaze met Connor's. "I'm his."

Connor shook his head.

Keegan's eyes gleamed with madness and power. *Just like our father's had.* "Want to watch her burn in front of you?" Keegan asked him.

His teeth clenched. "You won't...do that..." Talking was getting hard. His beast wanted out and that fire was choking him. The flames were so hot. If they didn't all get out of there soon, they'd be dead.

If we were humans, we'd already be dead.

The air was too hot. Humans couldn't breathe it and live.

Chloe swayed in Keegan's grasp.

"You're going to die here, Connor," Keegan said. "I'm going to watch you. You're going to stand right there and burn. Because if you move, if you take one step, I'll kill Chloe."

And Chloe...

Smiled?

"I'll kill you..." Keegan coughed a bit on the smoke. "Then I'll kill Duncan. I'll take out the whole Para Unit—"

Chloe's hand was rising. Had Keegan not even noticed that movement? Her hand was rising and her claws had come out. She stared at Connor and said, "I love you."

Fuck. Eric's idea had actually worked. Connor's compulsion was holding for her. Keegan couldn't control her. He couldn't—

Chloe spun in Keegan's grasp and she drove her claws right into his eyes. He howled and blood flowed and Chloe kicked him, sending him stumbling back into the flames.

Connor rushed forward. He swung out with the chains, slamming them into the side of Keegan's head. Keegan crashed into the floor. The floor gave way beneath him and he fell, going down in a ball of flames as he crashed into the basement.

Hell, yes. The fire was destroying the bastard — and not even a super vamp could survive those flames.

Chloe wrapped her arms around Connor. She held him tight. Her body trembled against his. "It worked! He was trying to get into my head, but I just kept thinking of you! Because I love you!"

More fire fell down on them. The whole building was shuddering and creaking and Connor thought the place would collapse at any moment.

They left Keegan and rushed for the door. Chloe stumbled so he just lifted her up in his arms, holding her tightly. He could see Duncan running toward him. The woman he'd rescued from the basement was out there. Eric was holding her. The vampiress fought his hold, but Eric wasn't letting her go.

The heat of the fire lanced over Connor's skin.

He reached the threshold. He heard the terrible groan over him. Connor leapt forward.

He and Chloe made it out. They fell to the ground, but they'd escaped! They'd gotten away from Keegan!

We made it. Chloe loves me. I love her.
We made it!

He reached for Chloe, and that was when Connor realized...the smell of blood coated Chloe.

"Baby?" he could see the wound on her neck, but...the scent of blood was so strong. Too strong. He hadn't noticed it before because the smell of smoke and fire had been too strong.

She was on the ground, staring up at the moon. He remembered how her legs had given way, right before they'd gotten out of that hell. He'd picked her up and run...

Why did her legs give way?

"Chloe?"

"H-he wanted me to...call out for you...wanted you to walk into...trap..." She licked her lips. "I didn't."

Her voice was too soft. Too weak.

She had on a dark coat and when he opened it with trembling fingers.

Then he saw her wounds.

"He kept cutting me..." Her voice had gone even softer. "But I...I didn't call out. Not until you saved her."

Her? The vampiress?

His gaze cut to the woman. She was staring at Chloe with stunned, desperate eyes. The vampiress wasn't struggling in Eric's arms any longer.

"Made him believe…I had given in…knew you had to come back up…the fire…too strong…"

"She needs help!" Connor roared.

His bellow shook everyone from their stupor. Eric freed the vampiress and ran over to them. Holly rushed from the right. Duncan fell to his knees beside Chloe.

Holly sucked in a sharp breath. "Oh, Connor…"

No, no, she didn't need to look at Chloe with such pity. She didn't need to shake her head.

He put his hands on Chloe's chest. He had to stop the blood.

"He cut her heart, Connor." Holly's voice was sad. "Don't you see? He cut into her heart."

"She's okay!" *She has to be okay.*

Chloe smiled at him. "I kept thinking of you. You…you said you loved me."

"I fucking do. Always." He put his hands down even harder on her wounds. "Get her some stitches! Give her some blood! Help her!" Because she couldn't die. He couldn't watch that. Not again.

"I'll…come back…" Chloe said.

"What if you don't?" His terrible fear. "What if I lose you? No, baby, no, just stay with me." They weren't helping her, so he picked her up and ran with her.

Shane and Olivia met him half-way. Shane's chest was also covered in blood and when Olivia reached for Chloe, he saw that blood stained Olivia's fingers.

"She dug the bullet out of my heart," Shane muttered. "And what the hell happened to your girl?"

Connor stared at Olivia's stricken face. "Keegan happened." Fear was choking him. "Make a wish, Olivia. Bring her back. Make sure she comes back."

Olivia's stark eyes met his. "My wishes don't work anymore."

She was growing cold in his arms. Barely seeming to breathe at all. "Make her come back! Wish her back!" And he ran on, pushing past them when tears slid down Olivia's cheeks.

"I wish..." Olivia's soft voice followed him.

There were medics up ahead. They could sew her up. He saw an ambulance to the right. Carefully, he lowered Chloe on the gurney near that ambulance.

Her eyes were closed.

"Chloe?"

She wasn't breathing.

"No, Chloe, don't leave me!" He would have traded anything for her right then. Any fucking thing. "Come back! Stay with me!"

The others gathered around him. No one spoke.

No one but...

The vampiress he'd saved. "She looks like her mother."

Connor didn't look at her. He couldn't take his eyes off Chloe.

"Her mother...was my friend. The only friend I had. Until that bastard Keegan killed her." She reached out her hand and smoothed back Chloe's hair. "I think she's still breathing."

No, she wasn't.

"Let's see if she's hungry."

Then she slashed open her wrist and put it over Chloe's mouth.

"No!" Eric shouted. He grabbed the woman and hauled her back. "What the hell are you doing? Chloe isn't human! She comes back!"

She should come back...but she wasn't.

"I wanted to help," the vampiress said, her words shaking. "The way her mother helped...I wanted to help..."

Blood smeared Chloe's lips.

"That's it!" Olivia's voice was excited. "It fixed me—it can fix her, too!" And she was grabbing a scalpel from one of the EMTs and slashing open her wrist. She put it to Chloe's mouth.

Connor shook his head. What the hell were they thinking?

"It takes a female vamp to make a cross-over, right?" Olivia said, her voice breaking with hope and fear. "Then let's make her a vampire. Let's fix it so she doesn't die! Let's—"

"Stop." Eric's voice was low and lethal. "You don't know what Chloe wants. She's been screwed with enough."

Olivia blanched. Her wrist was still over Chloe's mouth.

Chloe wasn't drinking her blood. Chloe wasn't moving at all.

Eric stared at Connor. "What would Chloe want?"

To be free.

His chest burned. The fire seemed to be rising inside of him. "I love her," he said. She needed to open her eyes. She needed to come back to him.

Olivia's hand fell away from Chloe. "I'm sorry," she whispered. "So sorry. "

Connor leaned over Chloe. "I love you so much, baby. Please, please, come back to me." *Because I don't think I can live without you.* "Just open your eyes and come back to me." She'd come back before—twice—within moments.

The first time she'd died, when her own father had killed her.

And the second time....when Keegan had broken her neck.

She'd come back so quickly.

"Why isn't she back yet?" Connor asked. The pain inside was growing worse. Spreading. Destroying. He needed Chloe. Needed her to open her eyes. Needed her to *see* him. If she would just open her eyes, just smile, then everything would be all right.

The minutes passed in painful silence. Eric's hand curled around Connor's shoulder. "You may have to let her go."

No. He shook his head. He wouldn't give up on Chloe.

She hadn't given up on him.

"She should have come back by now," Eric said, voice gruff. "Let's get her back to the base. Back to the lab there. Let's —"

Chloe's eyes flew open.

Connor nearly hit the ground. He grabbed for the gurney. Grabbed for Chloe. He yanked her into his arms and held her as tightly as he could.

Her arms were around him. Holding him. Squeezing him just as fiercely as he squeezed her. He could feel her heart beating. He could hear her breathing.

She'd come back.

Tears stung his eyes and he didn't fucking care. He had Chloe.

He had his life back.

He kissed her. Wildly. Desperately.

"I'll be damned," he heard Eric say.

Yeah, the guy would be—but that wasn't a problem Connor needed to deal with right then.

He stood up, holding Chloe in his arms. He didn't think he'd be letting her go anytime soon. But he pulled his lips from hers, just long enough to whisper, "I love you."

She smiled at him. "And I love you."

He kissed her again and Connor knew that he would never, ever let Chloe go. She was more than just his mate. She was his soul and without her...

He was a beast.

She made him a man.

***

Something was wrong.

Chloe stared at her reflection in the bathroom mirror. She couldn't put her finger on it, but something just seemed off.

Probably a side effect of dying...and coming back. Again.

But...she felt different. Kind of hungry.

Kind of horny, too.

Hmmm...where's Connor?

She turned off the light and headed back to her little room at the base. They would be getting better accommodations, ASAP, but for the moment...

Connor stretched in the bed, and he smiled at her. He was naked. His hair was tousled, and he was so sexy.

She smiled at him.

Connor blinked. "Um, baby..."

She slid into the bed with him. Put her body against his. The guy was so amazingly, deliciously warm. And he was all hers! No more fears, no more bad guys...they were safe.

She kissed his neck. She could feel his pulse pounding beneath her lips. Such a fast, strong beat.

Her teeth scraped lightly over his neck. He growled his pleasure.

She was naked. So was he. Why bother with foreplay? She wanted him.

Right then. Right there.

Chloe straddled him. His fingers slid between her legs. Pushed into her. Had her gasping against his neck.

Her teeth raked him again.

He thrust into her.

Yes!

Pleasure spiraled inside of her as he thrust and thrust, and she bit down on his neck. The move of her mouth was instinctive.

His blood spilled onto her tongue. Heaven, paradise, wine. *Connor.*

She drank from him and the pleasure nearly tore her apart. So strong she couldn't breathe. So powerful it overwhelmed her. She shuddered. She quaked. She came until she thought her body would collapse.

And Connor was with her, roaring out his pleasure. Riding that endless wave with her.

She licked his throat.

Chloe felt the drumbeat of his heart against her.

She felt him getting thick and long as his cock stretched inside of her once more.

Oh, yes, please…

"Baby…" Connor's voice was a growl. "Something you should know…"

She wanted to fuck and she wanted to bite.

She also wanted to love him. Forever.

"I don't think…you're just a werewolf anymore."

Her head lifted.

He touched her fang. "Baby, you're a vampire."

Her jaw dropped. Chloe shook her head.

He nodded. "You are."

Her hands clamped over her mouth. *I took his blood. I drank it — definitely vampire-style.* She stared at him in rising horror.

"Olivia and that other vampiress…they tried to give you blood at the scene. You weren't waking fast enough," Connor shook his head.

"They changed you. I didn't think it was possible. I mean, normally, a vampire has to take the blood and give it—" He broke off as his eyes widened. "*I* took your blood. Several times. Oh, Chloe, baby, I'm sorry!"

I'm a vampire?

Her hands slowly lowered. If she was a vampire, then she'd have to worry a whole lot less about the dying and coming back routine. "Do you mind?"

Connor cupped her cheek in his hand. "I love you. Vampire. Werewolf. Djinn. I wouldn't care what you are, baby. The only thing that matters to me is that you're mine."

And the only thing that mattered to her…*still being with Connor.* Actually having a chance to be happy with him.

If she truly was a vampire, then they wouldn't have just a chance together. They'd have forever.

He pulled her back down toward him. Connor kissed her lips. "I'll be with you," he said softly, "by your side, no matter what comes."

That was exactly where she wanted him to be. "And I'll be by your side." She pressed a kiss to the line of his jaw. "Always."

When she slept later, Chloe didn't have nightmares, but she did have dreams.

Dreams of her new life, with Connor.

I'll always choose to stay with him.

EPILOGUE

"Let's go over this one more time," Eric said as he rubbed his chin. "Tell me *exactly* what you wished, word for word."

Olivia squirmed a bit in her chair. "My wishes don't matter. You said that. I-I'm a vampire now, so—"

"Humor me," he said, forcing a smile.

Olivia glanced over her shoulder at Shane. Eric knew he had to tread carefully when Shane was around. The vamp wouldn't like it if he jumped across the desk and shook Olivia in order to make her talk.

Not that he would do that.

Yet.

Chloe shouldn't have become a vampire. That's not the way the transformation worked. Only, she had. Holly had conducted the tests to prove that fact.

"The words were actually Chloe's," Olivia said as she shifted some more in her seat. "She said something like...'*Are you sure you don't have another wish in you?*'"

He waited.

"I didn't think I had another wish in me," Olivia mumbled.

His fingers tapped on the table.

Olivia bit her lip. "She asked... *'Maybe one that makes me indestructible and lets me live forever with the man I love?'*"

Hell. That would do it. "And you said...?"

Olivia looked down at her hands. "I told her that I wished I could do that for her."

Oh, I think you did, Olivia.

He glanced over at Shane and found the vampire glaring at him.

"Did I do it?" Olivia asked, voice hushed.

"Either you did with your wish or with your blood." And that vampiress had helped, too. He currently had the mystery vamp in containment, but that would be ending soon. He needed to talk more with her, but every time he got near the woman...

There is something about her. She puts me on edge.

He would study her more. Learn her secrets. Figure out how the hell she'd wound up—according to Connor—chained in Keegan's hell.

But, he'd take things one at a time. For the moment, he had another victory, of sorts, to savor.

Shane and Olivia slipped from the office. He'd have to watch Olivia very carefully. If another wish came true, then they could truly be screwed.

A djinn had too much power, and there was no way he could let one run unchecked in the world.

He turned on his laptop. Keyed up the security feed. And there *she* was. The vampire they'd found. The woman with the light blue eyes and the face that was eerily perfect. The woman who—

She stared up at the video camera. Looked into it as if she could see him.

Impossible, of course. She had no idea who was watching her.

But then…that vampiress lifted her hand. She pointed at the camera—*at me?*—and said, "Come to me."

He started to rise, but Eric caught himself. What the hell? He danced to no one's tune.

No one.

He would uncover that woman's secrets. Every single one of them.

###

A NOTE FROM THE AUTHOR

I appreciate you taking the time to read CHARMING THE BEAST, and I hope you enjoyed Connor's tale. I've really enjoyed writing my Purgatory books. I hope to release a story for Eric Pate very soon!

If you'd like to stay updated on my releases and sales, please join my newsletter list www.cynthiaeden.com/newsletter/. You can also check out my Facebook page www.facebook.com/cynthiaedenfanpage. I love to post giveaways over at Facebook!

Again, thank you for reading CHARMING THE BEAST.

Best,

Cynthia Eden

www.cynthiaeden.com

Don't miss the other books in the Purgatory series.

THE WOLF WITHIN

FBI Special Agent Duncan McGuire spends his days–and his nights–tracking real-life monsters. Most humans aren't aware of the vampires and werewolves that walk among them. They don't realize the danger that they face, but Duncan knows about the horror that waits in the darkness. He hunts the monsters, and he protects the innocent. Duncan just never expects to become a monster. But after a brutal werewolf attack, Duncan begins to change...and soon he will be one of the very beasts that he has hunted.

Dr. Holly Young is supposed to help Duncan during his transition. It's her job to keep him sane so that Duncan can continue working with the FBI's Para Unit. But as Duncan's beast grows stronger, the passion that she and Duncan have held carefully in check pushes to the surface. The desire that is raging between them could be a very dangerous thing…because Holly isn't exactly human, not any longer.

As the monsters circle in, determined to take out all of the agents working at the Para Unit, Holly and Duncan will have to use their own supernatural strengths in order to survive. But as they give up more of their humanity and embrace the beasts within them both, they realize that the passion between them isn't safe, it isn't controllable, and their dark need may just be an obsession that could destroy them both.

MARKED BY THE VAMPIRE

Vampires exist. So do werewolves. The creatures that you fear in the darkness? They're all real. And the baddest of the paranormals…those who love to hurt humans…they're sent to Purgatory, the only paranormal prison in the U.S.

His job is to stop the monsters.

Deadly forces are at work within Purgatory. The monsters are joining together — and their plans have to be stopped. FBI Agent Shane August, a very powerful vampire with a dark past, is sent into the prison on an undercover assignment. His job is to infiltrate the vampire clan, by any means necessary.

She wants to help the prisoners.

Dr. Olivia Maddox wants to find out just why certain paranormals go bad. What pushes some vampires over the edge? Why do some werewolves turn so savage? If she can understand the monsters, then Olivia thinks she can help them. When she gets permission to enter Purgatory, Olivia believes she is being given the research opportunity of a lifetime.

Olivia doesn't realize that she's walking straight into hell.

To survive, they have to rely on each other.

When the prisoners break loose, there is only one person — one vampire — who can protect her, but as Olivia and Shane fight the enemies that surround them, a dark and dangerous passion stirs to life between the doctor and the vamp. Shane realizes that Olivia is a woman carrying secrets — powerful, sinful secrets. Secrets that a man would kill to possess.

And Olivia realizes that — sometimes — you can't control the beast inside of you. No matter how hard you try. Some passions can push you to the very limits of your control…and the growing lust that she feels for her vampire…it's sending her racing right into a deadly storm of desire.

Welcome to Purgatory…a place that's a real hell on earth…

ABOUT THE AUTHOR

Award-winning author Cynthia Eden writes dark tales of paranormal romance and romantic suspense. She is a *New York Times, USA Today, Digital Book World,* and *IndieReader* bestseller. Cynthia is also a two-time finalist for the RITA® award (she was a finalist both in the romantic suspense category and in the paranormal romance category). Since she began writing full-time in 2005, Cynthia has written over thirty novels and novellas.

Cynthia is a southern girl who loves horror movies, chocolate, and happy endings. More information about Cynthia and her books may be found at: http://www.cynthiaeden.com or on her Facebook page at: http://www.facebook.com/cynthiaedenfanpage. Cynthia is also on Twitter at http://www.twitter.com/cynthiaeden.

HER WORKS

Paraonormal romances by Cynthia Eden:
- BOUND BY BLOOD (Bound, Book 1)
- BOUND IN DARKNESS (Bound, Book 2)
- BOUND IN SIN (Bound, Book 3)
- BOUND BY THE NIGHT (Bound, Book 4)
- *FOREVER BOUND - An anthology containing: BOUND BY BLOOD, BOUND IN DARKNESS, BOUND IN SIN, AND BOUND BY THE NIGHT
- BOUND IN DEATH (Bound, Book 5)
- THE WOLF WITHIN (Purgatory, Book 1)
- MARKED BY THE VAMPIRE (Purgatory, Book 2)
- CHARMING THE BEAST (Purgatory, Book 3)

Other paranormal romances by Cynthia Eden:
- A VAMPIRE'S CHRISTMAS CAROL
- BLEED FOR ME
- BURN·FOR ME (Phoenix Fire, Book 1)
- ONCE BITTEN, TWICE BURNED (Phoenix Fire, Book 2)

- PLAYING WITH FIRE (Phoenix Fire, Book 3)
- ANGEL OF DARKNESS (Fallen, Book 1)
- ANGEL BETRAYED (Fallen, Book 2)
- ANGEL IN CHAINS (Fallen, Book 3)
- AVENGING ANGEL (Fallen, Book 4)
- IMMORTAL DANGER
- NEVER CRY WOLF
- A BIT OF BITE (Free Read!!)
- ETERNAL HUNTER (Night Watch, Book 1)
- I'LL BE SLAYING YOU (Night Watch, Book 2)
- ETERNAL FLAME (Night Watch, Book 3)
- HOTTER AFTER MIDNIGHT (Midnight, Book 1)
- MIDNIGHT SINS (Midnight, Book 2)
- MIDNIGHT'S MASTER (Midnight, Book 3)
- WHEN HE WAS BAD (anthology)
- EVERLASTING BAD BOYS (anthology)
- BELONG TO THE NIGHT (anthology)

List of Cynthia Eden's romantic suspense titles:
- MINE TO TAKE (Mine, Book 1)
- MINE TO KEEP (Mine, Book 2)
- MINE TO HOLD (Mine, Book 3)
- MINE TO CRAVE (Mine, Book 4)
- FIRST TASTE OF DARKNESS
- SINFUL SECRETS

- DIE FOR ME (For Me, Book 1)
- FEAR FOR ME (For Me, Book 2)
- SCREAM FOR ME (For Me, Book 3)
- DEADLY FEAR (Deadly, Book 1)
- DEADLY HEAT (Deadly, Book 2)
- DEADLY LIES (Deadly, Book 3)
- ALPHA ONE (Shadow Agents, Book 1)
- GUARDIAN RANGER (Shadow Agents, Book 2)
- SHARPSHOOTER (Shadow Agents, Book 3)
- GLITTER AND GUNFIRE (Shadow Agents, Book 4)
- UNDERCOVER CAPTOR (Shadow Agents, Book 5)
- THE GIRL NEXT DOOR (Shadow Agents, Book 6)
- EVIDENCE OF PASSION (Shadow Agents, Book 7)
- WAY OF THE SHADOWS (Shadow Agents, Book 8)

Made in the USA
Middletown, DE
03 April 2016